CRUEL ANGELS
PAST SUNDOWN

HAILEY PIPER

Cruel Angels Past Sundown
Copyright © 2023 by Hailey Piper
All rights reserved.

Published by Death's Head Press,
an imprint of Dead Sky Publishing, LLC
Miami Beach, Florida
www.deadskypublishing.com

First U.S. Edition

Cover Art: Justin T. Coons
Edited by: Anna Kubik
Copyedited by: Kristy Baptist

The "Splatter Western" logo designed
by K. Trap Jones

Book Layout: Lori Michelle
www.TheAuthorsAlley.com

ISBN 9781639511273

PRAISE FOR
CRUEL ANGELS PAST SUNDOWN

"Piper is a voice to be reckoned with."

—Gabino Iglesias

"*Cruel Angels Past Sundown* is a gorgeous, bloody, surreal nightmare with a palpable, pulsing heart. Piper's innovative prose is tactile and immersive. It binds you to Annette's soul and the people of Low's Bend and makes you want to fight for them. By the end, I knew neither the wrath of heaven nor hell had any chance of breaking the bonds of queer love and found family. Long live queer horror in the face of those who would call us blasphemous. Thank you for this battle cry in the darkness. This book is a treasure."

—Suzan Palumbo, Nebula Finalist

"From its unforgettable opening to its furious, apocalyptic climax, *Cruel Angels Past Sundown* moves with the implacable dread of a nightmare. But the slashes it leaves in your gut, and the hardpan dust it rubs in the wounds, are all too real."

—Nat Cassidy,
author of *Mary: An Awakening of Terror*

to Sergio Leone and Ennio Morricone
with admiration and love

ONE:
SABER

THE WOMAN BEGAN as a hazy pale stalk in the distant prairie with a gleam beside her catching the sunshine, and that was everything Annette Ruthie Klein could make out from beside the grooved wooden fencepost.

She had been approaching Big Pete's pen when the light-on-metal glint caught her eye. Her brother Henry used to mind the old bull, but he had gone the way of Mother's sickness, and half the cattle herd had followed. Between Annette and her husband Frank, they had both needed to toughen, open up, and reach some understanding, or else let the ranch collapse around them. Annette did most of the coming and going, and sometimes Frank went with her, rarely by himself.

No visitor had come to the ranch since that last futile stop-in by Dr. Hastings, and they had followed him out with Mother's body in tow.

No visitor until this woman came staggering in from nowhere.

Annette eyed Big Pete beyond the fencing, a tired black bull with a lazy disposition. He didn't eye Annette back, only huffed and grazed and swatted flies with his swinging tail. By the time she tore her gaze again to the pale strip on the prairie, the woman had stepped closer and sharpened to a clear shape. No more a stalk against rough brown soil and patches of brush, but alive and human.

1

In her right hand, she clutched a cavalry saber, its steel blade blinking the last of the daylight. She wore no dress, no hat, not a scrap of clothing on her. She was too fair to have been walking in this sunshine naked—no tanning like Annette, no reddening—as if her saber had deflected every ray of sunshine.

And she was pregnant, skin stretched around a smooth round belly, heavy with child. Her bent posture said she felt the weight.

"Frank?" Annette called, letting go of the fence post. "Something ain't right."

What could he do? She wasn't sure, but he needed to know someone had come to the ranch.

If only Annette had gone to town today. If only she had spent yet another night in a room that wasn't hers.

The sky swelled red, the sun dipping behind distant western mountains. The naked woman seemed a white slit in a strange cat's eye, nearer now, nearer, almost to the fence. In moments she would be close enough for Annette to reach out and touch.

A huffing moan quaked through Big Pete's mountainous bulk, and he retreated from Annette to find surviving patches of brush on the far side of his pen. Wasn't she supposed to put him somewhere? Pasture, barn, the moon—clear thoughts sweated and mixed together. Her wide straw hat might guard her scalp and skin from the sun, but not her mind.

Or was the trouble this woman, now five steps away? The sight of her was making Annette dizzy. Did she want Annette's dull blue dress to cover her nakedness, to tear it away and reveal Annette's leathered skin and taut muscle? Except Annette had to be the stronger of the two. The woman was almost skeletal, her limbs and torso thin except at her belly. Either she was three months along and only showing for her thinness, or she was nine months along and her unborn child had taken to drinking and devouring everything but her skin and bones.

2

Annette was healthier, fitter, and didn't need clothes, or food, or home. She should give everything over and let this woman take her place at the ranch.

"The hell's with her?" a deep voice asked.

Annette hadn't heard her husband approaching. Frank Klein was a man born grown and aged, his exhaustion an inherited part of his soul. He wore a dark blue shirt, its buttons sewn by Annette's hand. His black mustache bent in a scowl as he turned from the pregnant woman to Annette.

"You know her?" he asked, his voice curious, ever-patient.

Annette opened her mouth, but her tongue was a flat dead animal behind her teeth.

Frank seemed to notice only now the woman was naked. His cheeks reddened, the most bashful man Annette had ever met, and he glanced away. "Lead her in," he said. "I'll fetch one of them blankets."

He was off toward the ranch house before Annette could ask how she would lead the woman. Her gaze crossed Big Pete again—wandering now—and then the woman stood right behind her. A mane of shaggy black hair haloed a narrow face with pursed lips, a small nose, and eyes leaning the yellow side of brown. They almost seemed to shine with the waning sunlight, the same as her saber.

Was Annette supposed to lead her to the barn? Had that been Big Pete? Her thoughts were melted butter down her spine. She stumbled back from the naked woman, nervous against touching that skin, likely hot as a sunbaked salt flat. The gleaming saber turned sideways, a bright smile over the soil.

"Come," Annette said, and she stumbled back another step. "Come along, saber girl." Except this woman was too grown to be a girl. A lady with her weapon, naked or not, deserved better than to be called after with a wave and a high-pitched tone as if Annette were leading reluctant cattle home.

3

But Saber seemed more animal than human, didn't she? Naked as a beast, quieter than Big Pete, only staring without end, her head full of wind and instinct.

Still, she knew enough to follow.

The ranch house stood with unpainted wooden walls and a leaning roof with its two chimneys jutting hornlike to either side. Its doorway often hung dark, neither Annette nor Frank bothering to light more than a wispy lantern near dusk anymore.

But tonight candles glowed along the supper table beyond the front doorway and kitchen, and more of them dotted the sitting room shelves to one side. Their small flames danced in Saber's eyes.

Frank appeared from the sitting room carrying a thick woolen blanket. He passed it to Annette, and she wrapped it around Saber's shoulders. Her arms dangled at her sides.

"Sit her down," Frank said, pulling out a wooden chair from the supper table—his chair, at the head. When Saber didn't move from Annette's side, he patted the seat with a thick, scarred hand. "Here, miss."

Saber shuffled toward the seat and collapsed onto it. Annette's mind boiled, but she pulled the blanket snug around their guest's front and covered her nakedness. Better than dressing her. That would be like fitting a shirt onto a wolf, but Annette had tossed blankets on the horses, cows, and even Big Pete. Had she left him outside or brought him in? She couldn't remember. Maybe he would act like Saber must have, shifting shape from beast to human. Any minute, he would wander inside, naked and silent, holding a horn in each hand instead of a sword.

Frank knelt beside Saber's seat. His bones creaked all the way down, and he had to set a hand on the table's edge to steady himself. He managed to look into Saber's amber eyes, her nakedness no longer so obvious.

"Got a name, miss?" he asked, gentle as the blanket.

Saber stared hard at the table as if her name were carved into its planks.

"Where you come from?" Frank shifted uncomfortably. "Someone take your clothes? Who did this to you?"

There was a strange ticking, and Annette hoped it was Saber's mouth slinging open to speak.

The tick came again, and Annette glanced under the table—the point of Saber's blade tapped the plank floor, up and down with her slow breath.

"How about that sword?" Frank asked. "Looks like cavalry issue from the war, what, twenty years back? Maybe your husband's? Or your father's? You're too young for it." He smiled, as if he thought Saber might laugh at his little joke, but she remained sullen.

Annette wanted to chuckle, felt it bubble in her throat, but she didn't have the strength for humor. Saber's head turned in steady inches, and her yellow gaze shifted across the candlelit room. She seemed to be looking anywhere for answers. Annette had none. She couldn't have even stood if Frank weren't here. Without him, the walls might turn to mud and then slop down to the floor, abandoning all shape. Through the windows, sunset purpled the world.

"You hungry? Thirsty?" Frank made to stand. "Powerful heat today, miss."

Annette's voice rolled out. "Saber." The blade no longer gleamed with reflected sunshine, but candlelight kept it smiling even in the dim ranch house. *Tick, tick.*

Frank glanced at the point as it tapped the floor again. "Wouldn't part her with it," he said. "That'd be like pulling out a cat's claws. She wouldn't hurt no one with that if she didn't have to."

A thin red teardrop traced down his cheek. The color had to be some trick of the light, but when he wiped it with his sleeve, a dark splotch stained his shirt. There was no impatience in the firm line of his mouth. His brown eyes lit with nothing more than an earnest desire to help this poor woman as red tears streaked down his face.

Didn't his heart hurt to stare into her eyes? His thoughts seemed solid enough to ask questions.

Annette couldn't say the same. Husband and wife alike usually came stiff and sturdy as fenceposts, standing firm after a storm when everything else had been blown away, no choice in it.

But not tonight. Annette had turned from a fencepost into a puddle of spilled milk, and Frank's demeanor seemed pillowy. He should have been aggrieved over Saber's full womb while Annette's kept empty—or was that Annette's expectation he might know her guilt?

They were due for a trip into town for some distraction, but distraction had come to them instead.

They supped on dry bread and the remains of an earlier chicken and leek stew. Annette kept dropping her spoon, her hands forgetting how to hold it. She didn't clean up either, not even to wipe the sticky fluid from her cheeks. Every step sloshed as if the floor teetered. She had never set foot on a ship, but her father had as a boy, he'd once told her when she was a child, shortly before his death. He had said the deck swayed up and down like they were sailing on a giant's chest. The ranch house did the same tonight.

Saber did not eat or drink. No cracked lips, no sunburn, no dry scaling on her hands. Like Annette and Frank had imagined this woman out of the spring wind, someone to bear children for them when they had none.

Was their absence because of him? Because of her? A mystery, but no matter the reason, Frank could never know her secret relief. He had accepted so much strangeness in her town trips, respected her needs, even joined her, listened to her, understood and bore it all, but to know she had never wanted his children would have hurt his heart, and this good man didn't deserve the pain.

If Saber brought them children, taking on the role of mother that Annette had never wanted, she would be a blessing more than a phantom. If it made Frank happy, she would welcome it.

Cattle lowed beyond the ranch house walls. Were they

out stalking the fences, or did they stand in the barn? Annette didn't know.

Frank spoke haltingly with a drowsy tone. "Annie. See what's. Fussing. Them animals. Would you?"

Annette wanted to ask why he was crying blood, or if she was crying as many red tears. The words wouldn't form. The cattle lowed again, demanding she mind them.

She wobbled to her feet and started for the front door, but her path skewed toward the sitting room's small square window. The crimson sun scarcely peeked over the western mountains, and every fencepost's shadow scraped claw-like toward the ranch house. That had to be what was spooking the animals. There were coyotes to consider, and sometimes wolves, but Annette didn't see them.

Maybe the predators, too, were frightened. She couldn't say why. The shadows might reach out and terrify every lean predator for a hundred miles.

She was frightened with them, but she couldn't say why.

The air sagged against the floor as she turned from the window. She dropped to her hands and knees. Wooden planks pressed her fingertips, but they'd turned muddy since she crossed the house. Lit candles glowed with purple-red auras, each a miniature dusk with its own drowsy sun. Red tears clotted Annette's eyes.

Her dreams had no firm skeletons to keep them standing, only flesh and tissue and bones, a collapsing cavern of innards without rhyme or reason. Nothing held real shape inside this red nightmare, but Annette found Saber's face and a raw, unnamable taste in her mouth.

The word came to her as she woke up—blood. She must have bitten her tongue when she hit the floor, though no wound stung when she ran its dry pad back and forth under her curious teeth. The taste lingered in her throat, a copper coin tossed into a campfire. She must have swallowed in her sleep, taking dreams, blood, and a mysterious wound down her throat.

The sitting room candles had gone out, leaving the house a black framework bracing moonlit windows. Did a hand brush her collarbone, or was that the wind?

Heat stirred in her chest, some of those melted thoughts pooling in her heart, her lungs, down, down. She couldn't tell where they ended, her body a bottomless channel along an infinite spine. She didn't want to tell.

A wet crackle iced her skin. Something shuffled in the darkness. Coyote? Wolf?

Annette pressed against the floor, inhaled the smell of dust, and then listened. She knew the general restlessness surrounding the ranch house. That was prairie life, all insects and wind, and coyote howls you hoped kept distant. Something was always loud and alive in the prairie night.

The crackle came again, a ticking. Saber's sword? No, too damp, a throat full of trapped air. Annette would have thought she'd swallowed a bubble of blood and made the noise herself, but the sound crossed the ranch house. She couldn't see what walked there, but she felt it break from one patch of darkness and scrape bare feet across the wooden planks toward the bedroom. Steel tapped the walls.

Annette rolled from flat on her back and onto her hands and knees again. She crept low through the hall, behind the moving darkness. Frank had been too tired and dizzy to notice she had passed out, but he must have made it to bed.

Where Saber found him.

She was a pale figure wreathed in blackness against the moonlight. That heavenly glow filled the bedroom as she approached the bed's foot, blade in her right hand, her flesh freed from the blanket.

So then, Frank was fond of this woman. Maybe because she showed proof in her very figure that she could give the children that Annette had not and didn't want to.

That was fine. Her heart trembled and her throat tightened, but she forced herself to swallow that tightness, remember hers and Frank's understanding, and accept this moment. He should have talked it out with her, but she was drowsy—it was fine. She, too, kept a piece of her heart elsewhere. There were nights he joined her in the boarding rooms above Slim's Respite in town, but there were nights she kept for herself and Gloria Travers, and Annette couldn't ask Frank for absolute faithfulness when she wouldn't do it herself. Besides, the bed offered plenty of room. They each had their needs and love. He must have whispered in Saber's ear to come find him after dark, while Annette slept on the sitting room floor, his good humor at last breaking through Saber's shock and silence.

Her round belly slid onto the bedding. Frank might pretend he was the man who'd impregnated her. Would she stay until the birth? Beyond? Would he and Annette help raise whatever slipped out between those white stick legs?

She should have asked, but right now she could hardly sit upright. One hand squeezed the bedroom's chipped doorframe, but it wouldn't help her stand. Every muscle tensed through her bowed legs, down her bent back.

Saber had no muscle like this. Her skin was an ash-white suggestion against the world, a dream allowed to walk the wakeful night. She crept onto the bed by hand and knee and saber, up Frank's legs, between them, to his chest. Her back arched, arms raised. Another wet crackle filled the room as her blade flashed a moonlit grin.

And then it sank into the warmest parts of him, painting dark streaks across its steel tooth.

Annette's hand let go of the doorframe and dropped over her mouth. A toad-like scream croaked and died in her throat.

"Annie?" Frank wheezed as if Annette could do anything to stop this.

His throat crackled, the same as Saber out in the sitting room, and his limbs jittered. One arm slopped off the bedside. Red rivers flooded the bedding, and then red waves. A familiar copper stink filled the air.

Saber jimmied her blade by the hilt as if rowing a boat down these bloody waters. Dark stains spattered over the pillows, headboard, and walls, all glistening in moonlit dots and ringlets down her once-unblemished skin.

The blade worked into Frank's chest and levered his ribcage up, a damp sun rising within the mountain of his flesh. Saber's free hand clawed into the stretched cavity, and her face lowered. A wet fat snake of a tongue uncurled through lips and teeth, long as her arm, and its tip hunted somewhere inside the open cavity. She must have been hungry after all.

Annette slipped from the doorframe. Flailing hands pawed at floor and wall, back and back until a surface touched her from behind and made her gasp—nothing worse than the wall opposite the doorway.

But she couldn't inhale the gasp like it had never happened.

Saber's tongue froze wet in the moonlight. Her free hand slid back, fingers tangled with dark, nameless lumps, and her face turned from the gory cavern. Her jaw worked back and forth. She might have been trying to speak, but she only managed a heavy groan, as if an aging wooden house had settled in her throat.

Annette shifted from the doorway's view and stumbled backward into the ranch house's darkness. She would become one with it, the way Saber had when she'd crossed from the sitting room to this freshly painted bedroom. Night's blanket would hide her.

Saber's wooden groaning followed Annette into the black. She staggered past the kitchen and supper table, out the front door. The sky blazed with stars and moon, and the world seemed less lonely when cattle lowed near.

Each step found firmer ground. Away from Saber, Annette stood straighter, and the muscles down her back and legs remembered they were strong. Her thoughts found their shapes again. She hadn't put Big Pete or the rest of the cattle to bed tonight, an absolute certainty she could lean on. Why had the inside of her home felt so murky? Why couldn't she think clearly when Saber stepped close?

Glancing back, the ranch house seemed solid and unshifting. It did not sail on a giant's chest in the way of her father's ship when he was a boy.

Frank couldn't be dead in there. Not with the rifles leaning by the sitting room fireplace and a shotgun loaded under the bed. His death must have been part of Annette's red nightmare and its copper tastes. She had dreamed a bloody cavern and then seen one in Frank's chest, same as when seeing a muzzle flare and then turning away shut-eyed, its ghost might stick behind the eyelids. She had only her thoughts to blame. What kind of repulsive woman dreamed of her husband's death?

But then, what kind of woman stood useless while another woman murdered him?

If Annette went back, she would know for certain, but only if Saber allowed it. Every thought might melt again the moment Annette stepped within five feet of that strange woman.

Turning west, away from the house, Annette looked into a brilliant star-dotted sky, an ancient place she might hide inside. She rubbed her cheek against her shoulder, scattering red crust across blue fabric, and thought she heard Saber's groan again.

If the red tears and the groan were real, wouldn't that mean Annette hadn't been dreaming? Or maybe a dream had thought her up instead, as if there were no such thing as Annette, only a consciousness she didn't understand, a dream older than its dreamer. Even dream places might sleep inside themselves. Deeper and deeper, like the thin layers of an egg, and what would hatch from inside now? Not Annette, already born twenty-nine winters ago. No tooth-beaked fluffy chick, either.

She heard the groan again and wondered what might nest in Saber's belly. Who was she? Where had she come from? Was there a father?

Did this new stranger know, approaching from the outer darkness?

Annette blinked, half-convinced she was dreaming him, too, and yet his shape persisted, emerging from shadows the closer he stalked across the western prairie. A heavy coat hung around his shoulders, partway hiding a black jacket and white shirt above stiff black pants. A round-brimmed black hat cast a shadow down his deep-lined, clean-shaven face. Old as Frank? No, a bit older. This man might have been a preacher, or a man who would steal a preacher's clothes.

His eyes stared much too blue for a desert night. Almost unreal, and yet the rest of him was solid. If dreams had birthed this firm man, they might birth all things, a nightly womb for God to create the world in secret.

The thought was strange—God had no womb, only almighty fingers—and Annette pushed it away as the stranger paused three paces from her. His thick boots ground the soil.

"You seem to have wandered from your place, little lamb," the stranger said. His voice was clear and crisp, the kind Frank said came to men who liked talking above anything else. "Not to worry. Men of God act as shepherds to mankind's flock, and we come well-suited for guiding lambs where they belong." He tipped his hat, and the shadow briefly deepened down his face. "Name's Balthazar Wilcox. This is the Klein ranch? You're Frank Klein's wife, yes? Tell me your name, child of God."

"Annette Ruthie Klein." She looked over her shoulder to the ranch house, and it stood darker than the sky and farther distant than she'd realized, little more than a squat outline beneath the moon. How had bad dreams ever chased her so far from home?

"Ruth," Balthazar said, weighing the middle name. "From the Bible. Did you know that?"

Annette turned to him again—two paces away—and shook her head. She had never heard the name Ruth mentioned in any Sunday sermons when she and Frank rode into town for church.

"I find kinship with Biblical Ruth. Like her, I'm a soul of unwavering faith." Balthazar took another step closer. "Perhaps I find kinship with you, too. Are you of unwavering faith, Annette?"

"I couldn't say." The night's chill crawled up Annette's arms as if it might warm itself in her dress. She wanted to tell it to find Saber if it needed warmth. She could melt the wind's thoughts.

"That's fine, just fine." Balthazar stepped again, and his scuffing boots kicked dust onto Annette's. "You're young, not yet a mother. It is your place to be fertile ground for the truth and the future. When you enter God's kingdom, there will be no sin to wash away but that of our forebears. You have faith in this, don't you?"

The moon's reflection now gleamed down a strange dagger in one hand, the blade as long as Annette's forearm. Balthazar's thick fingers partway hid the grip, but two arms stretched to either side of the hilt, and a head bulged between. The dagger had been fashioned from a wooden carving of Christ nailed to the cross.

The chill sank beneath Annette's skin. She could still be dreaming, but that felt like wishful thinking. None of this moment dribbled as formless as every second she'd spent with Saber. This man stood rigid as mountains and endless as the sky.

His coat billowed when he leaned toward her. "What might you be doing outside your house tonight?" His hand hefted the crucifix-dagger.

Annette tried to speak. Words had been easier, like thoughts, since she left Saber. Or since she forgot the dream of Saber.

But only a strange croak slipped up her throat.

Light flickered in Balthazar's eyes, the moon no longer wishing to know their brightness. "Where did you hear that?" he asked.

"I ain't sure," Annette said. But she was. The sound

must have drawn him. He'd come from the same direction as Saber, toward Klein pastures and fences and the ranch house. "Did you dream her?"

Balthazar didn't seem to hear the question. He stood to his full height, a pillar of a man against the bright sky. "She has set her pale mark into you. That is a shame. She keeps the hope, but she wears a sin nearly from the time when stars were young and men knew not dreams nor speech nor pain. Original sin reaches roots through us all, and you are pregnant."

Annette gaped to say not her, never, Saber was pregnant, but no words came.

"Pregnant not with child but with sin," Balthazar said. His dagger's blade glinted, catching the moon. "It is in you, and upon you."

He wasn't making sense. He knew about Saber, so why talk to Annette? Why waste his time? She needed to turn around and go home. No more dreams or strangers.

Balthazar raised a calloused hand, and his voice was steady. "As Gabriel once spoke to Mary of Nazareth, mother of God, be not afraid. I'm not disappointed in you. She has sensed trouble in your soul and shared it, my lost little lamb. You are not the first."

Annette stepped backward. One shoe caught against a mound of dirt, and her voice shook when she stumbled. "I ought to head home." She glanced over her shoulder again. The ranch house still stood at some distance.

"Indeed, you long for your husband's house, but our great father above calls us children home," Balthazar said. "I would see you answer God's call before any other."

Annette turned from the ranch house to Balthazar again, and the chill devoured her heart.

Tears rolled down Balthazar's cheeks. "You are blessed tonight, Annette Ruthie Klein."

His arm snapped toward her and plunged the crucifix-dagger into her chest as a creaking groan rang through the night. He jerked at the last moment, distracted.

CRUEL ANGELS PAST SUNDOWN

Annette's hands jittered toward her chest as he pulled the blade free. Her fingers ran warm and sticky. Stern muscle sagged beneath her and yanked her to the earth. The world squeezed into tiny points of light in a black fog.

Balthazar gave a haggard sigh, muttering under his breath. He strode past Annette and toward the ranch house. His footsteps thudded hard in her ears. "What's she found now?" he asked, maybe to the wind.

Annette stared at the dimming ground, heart thrumming. She could still breathe. So long as she lived, she could step. Move. Try.

She staggered up from the earth, one hand bunching her torn dress around the chest wound, the other swiping at the air for something to grab onto and steady herself. Her palm slapped wood, found a latch, and loosened it. A gate creaked open, and its groan sent her shaking, too much like Saber's throat while her hand and sword had dug beneath Frank's ribs.

Annette's chest screamed, shooting cold sweat down her skin. This was no dream. Any simple nightmare would be a relief.

A bulky shadow stirred ahead of her. She forced one foot forward, and then the other. She wondered if Balthazar had stabbed Saber before she came to the ranch, and that was why she walked like she didn't know how. Nothing seemed certain anymore. The whole world bled a melted slush of sticky fluid, creaking throats, and steel in flesh.

Annette's hand settled on thick, bristly hair matted across corded muscle, and she clambered onto a warm mountain. The bright moon she'd watched bathe her bedroom was a stranger now, an eyelid closed over its light, at least to her. A beast walked beneath her in this new dark, and she could only hope it wanted to flee as badly as she did.

TWO:
THE BLOOD AND THE BULL

RESTLESS STARS CRAWLED between Annette's narrowed eyelids. They sometimes snuck through the slits and haunted the blackness beneath. Other times, her eyelids shut deep, locking her in worse places than the dark, where the red nightmare painted Frank's insides through her skull. Here and there, Saber's pale face emerged from this tarry pool of gore, as if she swam the back of Annette's thoughts.

And then Annette would thrust her eyelids open a crack and see the stars again. She had to keep awake, or else the dreams would drag her into Frank's opened chest.

If she slept, she couldn't escape her hunters.

She felt them behind her. Wolves, coyotes, could be cougars, too. And worse. She might be riding some monstrous beast that heaved each muscle onward like a man pushing a boulder up an impossible hillside. Her world swayed, and she thought she might have wandered back inside the ranch house, with her husband's body, and croaking Saber, and Balthazar preaching over them, eyes closed to the new copper-scented paint.

But Annette had left the house behind, and only Big Pete lumbered beneath her. She'd found the black-haired bull by some miracle in the dark, and now he carried her along the southbound road. Had she found one of the horses, they might have galloped too hard at blood's scent and thrown her off.

CRUEL ANGELS PAST SUNDOWN

Big Pete was in no hurry. From town talk, riding him shouldn't have been this easy, but he wasn't like other bulls. Ancient and tired, he didn't shrug off the burden. His path bent around a brief dark shadow—some small hill?—and warm auburn light dotted the distance.

Annette let her eyelids sink with a smile. Nothing hunted her, not preachers, predators, or the damned. Balthazar was right from the start. He had stabbed her in cold blood with his crucifix-dagger, and somehow that tool had lightened her soul enough to climb toward God's domain.

No more guilt for what she used to do behind the locked doors of Slim's Respite when she would make excuses to Slim behind his bar, tip her hat to him in heading upstairs, and slide into another bed for an hour, or two, or too many. No more shame that Frank had joined her. No more heartache when she pretended remorse each time he longed to see her belly swell with their future children.

Unless her soul might be found unworthy. What sins remained in it? Had she mourned Henry and Mother right? Her father, too, dead these many years? Or might their souls be whispering in Christ's ear, *Not Annette, not my sister, not our daughter, don't make us spend eternity with the likes of her.* Or maybe God's will worked like Arch Bower said, that drunken Calvinist, preaching through a whiskey bottle that all fates had been decided at the beginning of time. Or his Catholic friend—Annette couldn't remember his name tonight—who once explained that everyone rested in their coffins until the world's end.

Heaven awaited, and Annette was almost there.

What would they say when she approached on a bull's back? She hoped Big Pete would be welcome in God's embrace. She hoped she would follow. Heaven must have seen worse than a stabbed young woman in a blood-spattered blue dress, her tawny hair matted damp and crimson down her severe face. The angels welcomed the tortured and mutilated and torn open across the centuries. Annette would be no shock to them.

Her eyelids shut out the stars again, and that red nightmare crawled onto her, into her, a thick coppery slug in her mouth. Nothing paradisical in this. A face drifted in the blood, but she forced her eyelids up at Big Pete's next step.

Sharp-edged silhouettes broke the light where wooden columns held awnings over squat porches. Glass glowed alive across broad windows. Most of the buildings ahead sat dark, but someone kept lanterns or candles lit. Was that singing Annette heard? Chatter?

She understood now. Big Pete was no horse, but he and the horses must have formed some rapport through the long nights, and they had taught him the ways they traveled. That, or he'd chosen the path of least resistance, a dirt road trailing south past the ranch and toward faint lamplight.

Toward people.

Had Annette come to Low's Bend at noon, the townsfolk would have gawked and gaped at her riding in half-dead and drenched in blood atop her ranch's big bull. Instead, she rode in on the dusk side of midnight, and no one walked the streets to point or cower or help her.

Except where Big Pete lumbered. In the glow of Slim's Respite, travelers and townsfolk alike could find drink, bed, and company. She hoped Dr. Hastings was staying for a late round.

She slid off Big Pete's back onto dry, flat earth. The landing shook her legs buttery at the knees, and she started to fall. One hand grasped Big Pete's hair. He grunted discomfort, but he didn't lash out, as gentle as Frank. She leaned into him, tensed her legs, and crossed two wooden steps onto Slim's flat porch. Boards creaked beneath her boots.

Two swinging doors waited for her to push them. The doorway looked narrower than she remembered, and she would have chalked it up to her swaying footsteps, but the light parted around flat boards—storm shutters. Slim expected bad weather soon and meant to keep that trouble out of his establishment.

Annette hoped she wasn't another kind of trouble. She leaned hard into the doors, swinging them inward, and collapsed into another nightmare.

THREE:
RESPITE

DARK WINDOWS SAID it was still nighttime when Annette again surfaced to the world. Scarlet curtains hung to either side of slender windowpanes, where a curious wind prodded the glass, but nothing came creeping into the dim room, lit only by a bedside candle.

She knew this place. Low's Bend, Slim's Respite, second floor, Treasure's room.

Annette rarely slept in this bed, or Sylvia's next door. When Gloria came to town, those were the overnight visits. Was she here now?

Annette made to sit up, but a gentle hand pressed her back. Flickering golden light framed two figures.

Sylvia kept her black hair braided back, and she wore a maroon corset and petticoat. Her lips pursed in worry down her russet-brown face as she aimed one dark eye at Annette. A black banded eyepatch covered beneath the other brow.

"Don't worry, Annie, you're safe," she said, but she didn't sound like she believed it.

Beside her, Treasure wore a blue corset and petticoat and cream gloves, almost as pale as her chalky skin. Dr. Hastings had said she had—what was it? Alb-something. Albert? Albatross? Words had turned to fireflies since Saber's coming, enchanting and yet slipping through Annette's fingers. Treasure kept indoors most days. Unlike Saber, she would burn in the sunlight.

"Dear, dear Nettie," Treasure said. "Oh, I'd sure hoped you might sleep the night. That was such a nasty scratch."

Annette lowered her chin to her collarbone. Her dress buttons were undone, her bloodied dress flayed open like a stretched skin, and a crude cloth bandage draped her left breast. A red-black stain soaked the center but had quit spreading.

A bandage shouldn't have been enough to help had Balthazar stabbed her deep, let alone all the way to her heart. But if she hadn't been passing out over blood loss, then why? Still adrift in her head over Saber? Or had Annette been too shocked seeing Frank's crimson-spattered body? If she was wrong about how badly she'd been hurt, she might have been wrong about his injuries, too.

She pressed Treasure's hand away and sat up. "Anyone else?"

"Anyone else?" Treasure fluttered dark lashes over pale green eyes. "Such as?"

The wind rattled the glass again, and Sylvia chinned toward it. "Frank?" she asked, and then yawned. She had likely been up all day, waiting and wondering at the roads. Few travelers came to Low's Bend of late. Neighboring ranchers and their families made up most of the small town's traffic.

Annette hoped there would be few travelers tonight too. Herself, Gloria if she was lucky, and no one else unless Frank had somehow survived and made his way to town. If anyone came hunting, then they knew they hadn't killed her. Saber or Balthazar, or both.

Treasure narrowed her eyes at the window and then turned to Sylvia. "See any lantern out there?" Sylvia shook her head.

A lack of lanterns meant nothing. Balthazar hadn't carried any light. Annette couldn't guess how he found his way, but the stars and moon were bright tonight and would keep that way unless those storm shutters she'd seen coming in had good reason to stand ready. Saber didn't seem to need light, either. The night didn't fight her, and the darkness was too happy to swallow her pallor.

"Either of you seen Gloria?" Annette asked.

Sylvia smirked, and her eye brightened.

"You ask like she wouldn't be in this room right now if we had, sweetheart," Treasure said. "She was due in this week, last I heard, but how's she supposed to know when she'll ride back? Could be tomorrow, or in two days. Hope she's in some town, not roughing it between. Mort tells Slim there's a dust storm rolling in."

Mortimer—now Annette remembered Arch's Catholic friend, much as two friends might argue over every conceivable subject. Words and thoughts would return to her the longer she kept away from the monster who'd come staggering onto her family ranch. The rest of her life, with any luck.

Boots tromped up the steps from the first floor. A familiar voice shouted he would be right back downstairs, and then knuckles tapped Treasure's door. She thrust a blanket over Annette's chest and swirled around in a flurrying petticoat as the doorknob turned.

"Dr. Hastings?" Annette called.

"No," Sylvia said, almost despondent.

Slim Santiago-Beltran stepped through the doorway, a narrow Mestizo man of angles and edges. A white button-up peeked through his dark vest and above his darker slacks. His black hair waved to one side as if following smoke from the thin cigar jutting along his smooth brown face. Hard eyes settled on Annette.

"How's it feeling?" Slim asked, with the smoky gravel of a young man trying to sound older.

Annette felt nothing. Covered by the blanket, she could almost believe she'd dreamed up the wound, Balthazar's strange dagger, and everything else since Saber had come to the ranch. But no one would come riding into town on Big Pete over any old nightmare.

CRUEL ANGELS PAST SUNDOWN

"How's my bull?" Annette asked.

Sylvia covered her mouth against a laugh.

Slim grinned around his cigar. "With the horses. They don't bother him, and he's no bother to them. We'll bring him back to your ranch tomorrow. Not sure how or why he got you here, though."

Annette set her jaw. They weren't going to believe her. She didn't believe herself. Calling everything a dream when blood had soaked her dress, steel had cut her skin, and her husband—her arms curled against her like a dead spider's limbs, as if taut muscle could stop memory.

Treasure sat at the bed's edge and tugged Annette close. "What's the matter, darling? You're looking sickly all of a sudden. We're gentle here, you know that."

Even this gloved hand made Annette scream beneath her skin. She was raw right now. Over steel? Or Saber? There was no knowing.

"Dr. Hastings?" she asked again.

"Hastings headed for one of the ranches a week ago," Slim said. "No sign of him since. Been that way for a few ranchers, too."

A week without the doctor. Strange, but not like he'd never been gone so long before. If she wasn't badly hurt, what could he do to help her anyway? She could stitch skin herself, but no one could stitch Frank's chest whole. If Dr. Hastings rode into town ahead of any storm and she brought him back to the ranch, he could only pronounce her husband dead.

Her chest stung when she began to cry. Treasure's embrace tightened, while Sylvia patted Annette's hair, some locks stiff with congealed blood. Slim chewed at his cigar and waited.

"Tell us," Sylvia said.

"You're with friends, you know," Treasure said, and then more insistent, "You *do* know."

Slim drew the door shut. Sometimes Annette overheard him telling Arch or anyone in the downstairs

23

saloon that Annette liked to come by and chat with the boarding room ladies, her husband too, and at Gloria's coming that Annette liked to stay up the night listening to stories of bounties, trades, and rough living in the wilderness.

Always fluttering around me, Gloria had said once. *My little butterfly.* And that name stuck, lending enough truth to Slim's excuses to seem like it was the whole truth,

But Slim knew there was more, as did Treasure and Sylvia. The walls of Slim's Respite were not thick. None of them could keep safe here without the others looking after them. Whether they were friends out of mutual protection, or that protection came from sensing kinship, Treasure was right—Annette was with friends. And tonight's evils were stirring in her chest, longing to be shared.

"We keep each other's secrets, don't we?" Slim asked. His flaring cigar seemed to wink a firelit eye.

Annette let out a harsh breath. She couldn't keep the terrible night locked inside, whether she wanted to believe it or not, whether anyone else believed it. And they would try their best to be here for her when Gloria and Frank could not.

In slow bursts, catching her words and trying not to let the world go dark, Annette told them.

FOUR:
STITCHWORK

THE SOAKED BANDAGE lay bare to Slim by the end of it. Annette didn't care what else he might see, only that he understood what Balthazar had tried to do.

"He must've meant to cut me deeper," she said, stroking two fingers over the rough cloth. "I thought he had."

"Preachers make poor killers," Slim said. "If he was really a preacher at all."

Balthazar had certainly talked the talk, but Annette doubted she could've gleaned the difference between preacher and pretender. She could hardly understand this room right now.

Sylvia kept pressing a white handkerchief to her cheek, while Treasure wrapped one gloved hand around Annette's fingers as if a hard enough squeeze might pull Frank from death and into Slim's Respite.

"Think he went hunting for that demon?" Treasure asked.

Annette cocked her head at the word. "Demon?"

"The woman," Sylvia said, and she began pacing the window, keeping watch for signs of travelers in the night. Candlelight glimmered off the tears in her eye.

"On Big Pete's back, it felt like she was following," Annette said. She watched the dark glass as if an ash-white face might peer through, but from where she lay, there was only Sylvia's dark reflection. "Or something followed, anyway."

Treasure tugged Annette's head onto her breast. "That awful man must've realized he didn't know his knife from his knees, and he was coming up behind that bull to finish what he started."

Annette couldn't know. She might have imagined any pursuer, drifting in and out of visions and dreams.

"Lord, watch over our friend Frank." Treasure glanced at the door. "We'll keep you safe, us and Slim."

"And Gloria, too, if she ever shows up," Slim said.

Pleasant campfire heat stirred in Annette's chest, and then sharp slicing guilt. She shouldn't be excited at the prospect of Gloria's coming when Frank was gone. Wasn't it wrong to want Gloria's comforting arms right now? Annette looked at her hands as if they had answers. They seemed faint in the dim light.

Slim plucked out his cigar and aimed at the door. "I need to keep an eye on the watering hole before those viejos downstairs start smashing bottles over each other's heads and lapping up glass and beer. Ladies, maybe we give her some privacy?" He nodded to Annette and then turned back to the hall. Groaning steps chased him downstairs.

Treasure and Sylvia made to leave, too. Sylvia patted her cheek dry again.

"I need a needle and thread," Annette said. "Black thread, if you got it."

"Practicing your needlework in the middle of the night?" Treasure asked. Sylvia pressed her arm, an insistent look in her eye, and Treasure dug through a drawer beside the bed. "Spool, needle—already threaded—and a thimble if you need. But I much prefer you'd rest, sweetheart."

Annette promised she would. She didn't know if she could keep that promise, but she would try.

"We'll be near," Sylvia said. She glanced out the window again and then wooden floorboards creaked along the second floor toward her room.

CRUEL ANGELS PAST SUNDOWN

Treasure watched the doorway. "Don't mind Sylvia," she said. "You know her. Always waterworks when someone's passed on. Even when the sheriff went, and she hated that man. I think she might've cried since he wouldn't be around to hate no more." She raised a gentle hand and turned to Annette. "Not that she'd ever hate your Frank. We were all fond of him. Especially Sylvia. Don't worry, I'll tend to her. And you."

These were kind words, but their fondness hadn't saved Frank any better than Annette's love. She nodded to tell Treasure she understood.

"I'd better get before I talk a bigger mess." Treasure retreated through the door. It closed over her soft expression, and then her steps padded down the hall.

Annette took a long, deep breath. Inhaling too far made her chest ache. She pressed her chin to her collarbone again and stared at the soaked bandage. Being left alone wouldn't heal the wound faster.

Neither would this room's memories. She recalled the first time she and Frank had both joined Treasure in this bed. They had come to town on errands, and Frank got to drinking downstairs while Annette found her way to the boarding room, her head aflutter with confusion and curiosity. Treasure's perfume had filled the air with flowers, as it filled her room now. Annette had worried she smelled too much of hay, dirt, and animal, but Treasure had waved those worries off. She had been patient and tender while Annette discovered the contours of a softer woman's body and liked them.

They had both been touching each other when Annette realized Frank stood in the doorway. Panic had been odd; she'd made to cover herself with this same blanket and couldn't remember why. He was the one man who had already seen her in the nude, and she had felt silly later that evening after the panicked rattle in her chest gave way to an altogether different thunderous rhythm.

After he'd strode into the room. After he'd closed the

door behind him, and taken off his hat and boots, and in the dim light, he had looked so thoughtful and innocent, Annette couldn't have been sorrier. He seemed born with a heart made for breaking sometimes. She reached for one weathered hand, squeezed his thick fingers, and then drew him close without realizing it. He didn't stop her.

They had never made children together, but that night they planted the seed of what they would call their *understanding*. Annette didn't have any other word for it, but sometimes when they returned to the boarding rooms, apart or together, Treasure's room or Sylvia's, an energy wove between them and filled their souls. Treasure had mentioned it, too. Sylvia hadn't, but there was a calm in her. These were secret places for wild and loving hearts.

Delicate, too, and changing, like when Gloria came into the picture, with her odd England quirks and bravado and glorious smile. And then when Gloria had eyes only for Annette. That time had strained Annette the worst, but right when she thought the fragile understanding might break, it held. So had Frank, still loved, still loving her. They had their needs and passions, and it was fine. Everything had been fine.

Until tonight. Now he was a knotted, twisted pattern in her head of shifting bone and spilled innards. Not a man anymore, but pieces.

"Why?" Annette whispered. "Why him?"

That was all she could get out before another bout of trembling and sobbing. There were still no answers when the crying finished. The tears must have forgotten them on their way down. Each time Annette shut her eyes, she saw the red nightmare, or worse, she saw her marital bedroom, and her husband prone across his bed, a Frank-shaped echo of slaughtered livestock with Saber hunched over him in the moonlight.

If Annette had to see blood, she would look on her own. Her fingers pinched the bandage and peeled it away in gooey strands.

CRUEL ANGELS PAST SUNDOWN

A lengthy cut opened the skin above her left breast, but Balthazar's crucifix-dagger had only scratched fat and muscle, nothing deeper. She had bled more than expected and could have sworn out there on the ranch that he'd driven steel within an inch of her heart, but despite the moonlight, the night was murky, and her thoughts and senses had been murkier.

Slim was right—preachers made poor killers, at least by blade. They were better suited to causing slow deaths, and a person might not notice they were the victim if the killing came by starving, suffering, or apathy. Frank had known that sometimes hearts found mending better in a little friendliness than in a sermon.

But this preacher could still do bodily harm, and Annette needed more than friendliness to mend her open wound. Candlelight stretched the needle's piercing shadow across the wall, longer than Saber's blade. Annette tugged Treasure's woolen blanket up alongside her chest, stuffed one corner in her mouth, bit down hard, and began threading her flesh together.

Needle through skin, thread following, through skin again, pulled taut. Every piercing hurt, but hers was the only flesh she could heal tonight, and she was going to see it done right.

Whenever Gloria rode into town, those dark, deep eyes watched her by candlelight, and their fingers traced each other's scars. Each told a story, some as mundane as the hot pan's burn on Annette's right forearm, others dangerous as the scaly line along Gloria's belly where her hunt for Tommy Quick sent a bullet grazing along her middle. There was warmth in those fingertips. The men downstairs could keep their jokes, like how too strong a woman was a battleax in the making, or how maidenhoods breaking on saddles meant a woman had rutted with a horse. They knew nothing of real ferocity and blood, or how passion thrived in the rooms over their own heads.

Frank was different. Better. And he deserved better.

29

Annette shouldn't have played forlorn when her womb never grew with child. Should have told him she was glad. She should have saved him tonight. Hadn't even tried. Saber had climbed onto that bed, and Annette had watched, cowering, and let it happen. Was Balthazar right, that she had been long pregnant with sin? She wouldn't become pregnant with anything else.

If she could have another moment with Frank, she would tell him the truth. All these secrets they had shared, and this she had kept to herself. Even when they quarreled, or worse, were silent, no matter which had started the fuss, he would always approach with a smile, or she would find him and tuck her arms around his waist from behind, and they would be good again.

And now he was dead. There would be no stitching him in a way that mattered.

The thread pulled her wound tight on the left side, and her breast formed an ugly grimace. One more scar for Gloria's fingertip to trace. Annette set the needle, thread, and thimble on the nightstand beneath the candle, spat out the blanket, and buttoned up her dress. She couldn't rest. Too many thoughts, and too many hours until dawn.

She glanced out the same window where Sylvia had been watching Low's Bend, but the dirt street gave no sign of Saber or Balthazar. No sign of Gloria either, and Annette hoped she hadn't run across either of those demons.

Outside Treasure's doorway, a candlelit chandelier hung from the ceiling, scarcely lighting the main room of Slim's Respite. A pair of oil lamps glowed along the second-floor railing. Annette sometimes wondered if Slim let the light go dim deep in the night to drive patrons out and let him close up, but more likely he did it for Treasure's sensitive eyes.

Neighboring doors stood shut down the hall from her room, and soft voices murmured behind Sylvia's door. Had she and Treasure been attending clients? No, they couldn't have left them then to tend to Annette. They had to be talking together over everything she'd told them, outside Slim's earshot where they could get their thoughts squared away.

Their conversation was none of Annette's business. She made for the stairs.

The scent of flowery perfume sank beneath an atmosphere of beer, sweat, and cigar smoke. Familiar, welcome odors. Anything was better than the coppery stink from the ranch house. A smooth banister slid toward the bottom of the stairs, where the corner table often kept brooding, road-weary men. Some of Treasure's and Sylvia's clients chose to wait there so they wouldn't have to cross the saloon once summoned upstairs.

Along the wall facing the staircase stood the entrance, an open doorway letting dry air flow around two swinging saloon doors. Dots of dry blood spotted the floor where Annette had collapsed. Tall shutters still leaned against the frame to either side, flat chunks of wood that could be moved to cover the doorway, each awaiting the dust storm. Past the entrance, an aging wooden piano seemed to grow from the far corner. Five round tables dotted the central floor, with plenty of seats between them. A few stools lined the sleek bar at the back of the saloon across from the entrance. Behind the bar, a doorway led to the kitchen, and a back door to the shed, stables, and whatever else Slim liked to hide on his property.

Arch and Mortimer nursed tall glass mugs full of beer and froth at the table nearest the entrance. Both men were bulky, beer-bellied, and clothed in cotton and dust. Annette couldn't remember Mortimer's trade, but Arch seemed to have a secret stash of coins keeping him alive since he never did much but drink, grouse, and wander around town.

Neither man glanced her way as she neared, but Mortimer leaned over the table and dragged fingernails over its scratched surface. "You don't know what you're on about."

Arch bared jagged teeth over his blond beard. "Pot to kettle, Mort."

Annette had caught the tail-end of some heated argument's long train ride, now reaching its station as both men launched up from their seats.

Mortimer pressed his hat tighter over his head. "You know, I got a Colt with six rounds, and your name's on every one of them."

"A Colt, you say?" Arch snapped. "I keep something a little bigger in the shed behind Slim's, by the make of Mr. Richard Gatling, and it'll rip you to tatters."

"Gentlemen!" Slim clacked an empty mug's glass bottom against the bar counter. "It's the middle of the night. You can argue over how many angels dance on the head of a pin in the morning, outside my establishment."

Arch and Mortimer sat down together, grumbling under their breaths to each other now that Slim had offered himself as a common enemy. Annette wanted to buy them drinks to keep the peace if she was going to be stuck here the night, but any coins lay in her money pouch back at the ranch. She left their table and approached the bar. The other tables sat empty.

Shelves lined the wall behind the bar, filled with glasses, bottles, candles, oil, and rope. Slim kept more supplies beneath the bar and in the shed out back. Low's Bend used to be a popular stopping place for travelers, headed to find ore, oil, and anything else that sounded better than home. Nowadays, it served the townsfolk, nearby ranchers, and anyone lost enough to wander through.

"Whiskey, if you don't mind," Annette said.

Slim glanced at her dress. Dried blood matted the tattered left side from chest to hem.

Annette sat hard on a stool and flashed urgent eyes. "Please?"

"Guess you'd need it more than anyone." Slim fetched a bottle and a small glass and began to pour. "I'm sorry,

Nettie. Come daylight, we'll get a couple of men together and head to your ranch, see what we can find."

Annette already knew what they would find.

Slim passed the glass across the bar into her hands. "I mean to do right by you. You've had a time of it. Drink that down, might help you rest."

"Resting is the last thing I want." Annette sipped from the glass and then tossed it back. A brimming fire at the bottom of her throat lapped greedy tongues at the drink. No more chill set into her by Balthazar's dagger.

She scanned the saloon again. No Dr. Hastings to tend her, as Treasure had said. No Gloria to distract with stories of bounty hunting across territories and states. She hopefully had found somewhere to settle in for the night, out of reach from demons, hellish preachers, and whatever storm Mortimer expected to roll across the prairie. No one sat at the piano and no one stood outside the swinging doors that Annette could see, though a man in a preacher's dark attire might blend with the night. The thick wooden storm shutters caught her eye again.

"I didn't see signs of bad weather," she said.

Mortimer looked up from his grumbling with Arch. "You weren't in no sense to tell shape from ship when you spilled in." He tapped the side of his beet-red nose. "Trust my senses."

"Didn't see any myself," Slim said, leaning close and notching his cigar into the ashtray. "But I've started a tradition where I humor men like Old Mort to make my life easier." He smirked, about to laugh.

Mortimer grunted. "Old Mort has seen more storms than you've seen women to bed. Each of you, you're just worried about Gloria, like those songbirds upstairs. For what? She handles herself aplenty, and besides, how's anyone to know when she's due in? Could be out by Monteau Station right now. Did she send a telegram? No, didn't think so. But a storm lets you know when it's coming."

Annette had overheard them talk about Gloria before. As if her coming in from Britain years back, wearing men's clothes, and hunting terrors across the prairie didn't make her interesting enough, these types needed to make up nonsense. Annette had given them plenty else to bullshit about, riding in bleeding on a bull, at least for tonight.

The porch outside groaned, and Mortimer shot up from his seat again. "There, see? Storm's here already."

"That's no storm," Arch said. "Someone's coming. Might even be Gloria."

"Not Gloria," Mortimer said. "Just weather. Plain old hard-hitting prairie weather."

Annette lifted the glass to her lips to drain any remaining drops and then set it down in front of Slim. Her chest felt hollow, ready to rot or burn. Likely not a good sign, but no need to say so.

"Prove it," Arch said, gesturing to the doors. "Glance out, she'll be there."

"You'll feel a fool, you wait," Mortimer said.

Slim tapped the glass with one finger and then raised the brown bottle. He would fill up Annette's glass much as she pleased tonight, maybe on the house. She only needed to decide if she wanted to drown her sorrows in a spirited pool or face her nightmares head-on. If she skirted them now, they might haunt her forever.

"You just wait." Mortimer stamped across the saloon toward the belly-level doors. They jittered lightly with the wind.

"It's Gloria," Arch said. "She must know Annette got here."

Another dry groan sank into Annette's ears, and every muscle tensed. That was no storm. It wasn't a weathered porch plank, either. She knew that creaking noise.

She swirled up from the barstool. "Don't go out there!"

Mortimer paused at the saloon doors, his hands resting on their curving tops, ready to push them open. A soft breeze batted thin strands of hair loose from beneath his hat. He began to turn, mouth open, a question or retort on his lips.

And then his jaw went slack like he had forgotten what he meant to say. The lids slid halfway over his eyes, and a bloody tear streaked down each cheek, carving a red line across his sun-chewed skin. He swiveled toward the doors, the night awaiting beyond, and pressed through them, letting the wood slap against his arms as they slackened to his sides. Another groan swallowed his footsteps onto the porch.

The meager light of Slim's Respite brushed faintly over a pale hand as it grasped Mortimer's shirt and dragged him stumbling into the dark.

FIVE:
THE DEMON

ARCH UNFURLED FROM his seat on shaky legs. "Mort?"

The saloon doors settled in their hinges. Above and below them, the night hung a black curtain over the world. No footsteps paced Slim's porch; no boots hit the soil. The wind slithered limp, alive but not yet the storm of Mortimer's prophecy. Only an uneasy creaking snaked through the doorway.

What stood beyond the saloon would raise her saber outside the light.

Arch twisted his head to the bar. "The hell was that? No way that white hand was Gloria."

Chalky skin filled Annette's head as she shot up from the bar stool. "Shutter that door!" she shouted.

"But—" Arch turned to the doorway and then back to the bar. His face creased from forehead to beard. "But Mort's out there."

"She'll kill us," Annette said. A familiar copper stink struck her nose. "Arch, shutter that door right now!"

Slim marched around the bar, his hands curling to fists. He glanced hard at Annette, reading her from trembling limbs to whatever expression crossed her face, and then rushed toward the saloon's entrance.

"Help me," he said, beckoning Arch.

"But who'll help Mort?" Arch staggered toward the door,

every jerky step echoing a naked pregnant woman bringing steely hell to the Klein ranch. "He hasn't screamed."

"Frank didn't scream either," Annette said. "He let her—"

She clapped both hands over her mouth as Slim turned questioning eyes over his shoulder. Dark red tears pooled beneath his irises and slithered along the creases in his face. Thin lines of blood painted Arch's cheeks, too, and slashed crimson streaks through his yellow beard.

Annette couldn't explain how she had seen this before. How Mortimer wouldn't put up a fight. How Saber must have lulled him into the same pleasing fog she'd thrown over Annette and Frank. And like Frank, Mortimer might even have the best of intentions.

And then Saber would raise her blade and repay his good deed.

"Shutter it," Annette said. Before Saber finished with Mortimer and came back for them. She let that part dribble down her throat. "Please."

Slim and Arch each pointed to each other's confused face. Realization came, and they grabbed the heavy tall shutters from beside the doorway and stuffed them side by side against the gap, hiding the swinging saloon doors and the night itself. Arch pushed his shutter to be sure it wouldn't fall through. Slim pulled a broad plank from beside the doorway and set it into two iron hooks on either side of the doorframe. If anyone tried to push the shutters from outside, the plank would brace them. Each stood taller than the doorway, and no one could pull them through without breaking them.

Was Saber that strong?

Slim tested the bracing plank against the hooks. He was breathing hard now, each step less sure than his last. A dry throat croaked over the porch, and Slim and Arch turned to the shutters as if they could peer through three inches of solid wood. They each pulled out red handkerchiefs and wiped the blood off their faces.

Annette pressed a hand beneath one eye and then the other—no blood. Either she hadn't stepped close enough to Saber this time, or she had already seen enough of the red nightmare that a second touch made no difference.

The shutters clacked against the bracing plank. The iron hooks held.

Arch shifted from foot to foot. "It's the wind. That's so, right?"

Slim took an awkward step back and wiped again at his face. "That's no wind."

The pressure relented from the shutters, letting the iron hooks cradle their bracing plank again. A *clunk-clunk* struck from outside.

"The doors," Slim said. Another backward step and he bumped against a round table edge and startled himself.

The unseen doors eased, gave another *clunk-clunk*, and then eased again. Annette thought she heard the hinges creaking, but there wasn't room for them to swing that far. No, this was another dry croak in a speechless throat. Frustrated and desperate, as much as raw instinct allowed. Saber wanted the people of Slim's Respite. Their insides and their tastes.

She wanted in.

Another tired wooden groan, and then porch planks creaked to one side.

Arch glanced left of the shutters to one dark window. "The glass?"

Slim gripped Arch's sleeve and tugged him toward the tables. "Don't get close."

Annette stared at one window. Night's curtain clung to the glass, hiding any hint of the dirt street or the darkened houses beyond. She waited for a suggestion of white to appear and then turn and press against the glass the way moths flew desperate toward lamplight, but nothing showed itself.

"But can it come through?" Arch asked.

"I don't think so," Annette said. "She's like an animal."

Except coyotes and wolves didn't wield steel. If Saber wanted to break the glass, she only needed her weapon's hilt. "Slim? Anything you ain't need that might cover the glass?"

Slim tried to take another step back and then spun around the table, heading for the bar. "Could pull the shelves, nail them over." He placed a hand on the top shelf where coiled rope and oil cans sat, and then he seemed to change his mind as he turned and reached under the bar. A messenger's gun slid into his hands, its side-by-side barrels gleaming in the chandelier light. "Got this Parker, too."

"For all the good it'll do," Annette said. "If she gets to us, we won't fight."

Shadows stretched and danced over the tables and floor as if Saber's prowling had rocked the ceiling chandelier. A draft had drawn air over the candles. Sylvia and Treasure peered over the second-floor railing, their faces forming cautious circles above.

Slim blustered from behind the bar and pointed up. "You two hide in your rooms."

Sylvia clutched the railing. "We'll be trapped."

"She's right," Treasure said, indignant. "Listen to her, Slim. Some trouble's lurking, and if it gets to the stairs, we got nowhere to go."

"Nothing gets past me, I swear." Slim cracked open the shotgun and checked for slugs. He looked satisfied and glanced across the saloon. "Nettie, you go, too."

Annette held in place. She was the only survivor of Saber's last arrival, aside from Big Pete. Would that experience do any good? Slim and the ladies had heard her story, knew how Saber walked and croaked and cut. They didn't understand the nightmare, but they would if she got inside.

She would suck them down a bottomless hole, drown their thoughts, and feed on their insides. She might have had her reasons for sparing Annette at first, but that didn't earn gratitude or mean she wouldn't change her mind this time.

Especially when Annette felt a furnace burning deep inside her. Beyond the drowsy cloud, her fingers itched to rend and tear.

Frank had not been a vengeful man, but wasn't that the sort who deserved some vengeance on his behalf?

Hard steel scraped outside the saloon corner, beyond the walls where the piano sat. Annette slipped around tables as another, louder scrape sent Sylvia and Treasure scurrying from the railing and back behind a closed door.

Saber had abandoned the front of Slim's Respite. The ground floor's only windows faced the front street; upstairs kept the only back-facing windows. No glass to let Saber in.

But there was another entrance.

Annette wheeled around and pressed against the wall. "The back door?"

Something clattered beyond the rear wall. Slim looked at Annette as if her terror could tell him what to do next, and then he dashed around the bar and through the doorway to the back room. Furniture scraped behind the wall, likely to block the unseen door.

The porch creaked again. Arch haunted the floorspace between the tables as if the noise were chasing him. "What should I do?" he asked.

Saber had been searching behind Slim's Respite; her staggering couldn't have already led her to the front again unless she'd sped up. Hunched down, bounding on all fours out of the dark—Annette shuddered the vision away. This demon would prowl round and round, keeping everyone trapped until morning. Maybe longer.

Who said demons hid from daylight? If Low's Bend awoke, its residents filling the street and going about their day, they might fall under Saber's spell together. No one would harm her, everyone drowsy, helpful, and vulnerable.

Knuckles knocked the wooden shutters from outside,

and their percussion slapped Annette flatter against the wall. Saber wouldn't knock any more than a wolf. Had Mortimer survived and come looking for shelter?

"Anyone there?" A man's voice came muffled through the wood. "I see your lights on. Might I come in? There's a brutality in the air, and the rest of town's a dark place."

Slim appeared as the knock came again and stood frozen behind the bar. Arch glanced over his shoulder. Annette didn't know what to do either. No one wanted to take charge.

Another knock and the voice came louder, clearer. "You wouldn't deny a man a warm place to catch his breath and wet his much-parched throat, would you?"

Annette crushed her spine against the wooden wall. She needed the saloon to drink her in, let her become part of it, not a creature of flesh but of boards and nails and corners.

She knew that voice. Saber had followed her to town, and so another had followed Saber down the southern road from the Klein ranch to Low's Bend, with a Christ-carved dagger in his coat.

Balthazar Wilcox.

SIX:
THE PREACHER

THERE WAS ANOTHER wooden scrape—Arch was halfway through pressing the bracing plank from the doorframe's iron hooks.

Annette peeled herself off the wall. "Don't."

"Can't leave him to that thing," Slim said. "Mort's gone, but this man has a chance."

The left shutter sank into Arch's grasp, and he dragged it to one side. Weathered hands reached through the doorway and clutched the other shutter's edge, each sleeved by a familiar black coat. One saloon door swung inward, followed by a boot, leg, and brim of a black hat.

Annette couldn't make it to the bar, back room, or staircase before Balthazar would stride in and spot her. She slunk toward the corner and dropped behind the piano. Its boxy frame blocked a cramped pocket, where she ducked low and curled up tight. An uncomfortable hiding spot, but she fit between the piano, wall, and grooved floorboards choked by dust.

Hard boots thundered across the threshold. "Thank you kindly, sirs," Balthazar said. "Had no meaning for trouble." Wood clacked after him—Arch had replaced one shutter, and now he slid the bracing plank into the iron hooks. Slim's Respite would keep Saber out.

And keep everyone else locked inside with a madman.

Annette peeked around the piano's corner and watched

42

CRUEL ANGELS PAST SUNDOWN

Slim tuck his shotgun beneath the bar as Balthazar approached, right when the firearm would have helped them.

He looked ordinary in the saloon's dim light as he drew off his brown coat and set it on a table, revealing only his dark preacherly attire. Not so imposing as when he had towered in the moonlight. An average man, any preacher wandering in from any town, on his way to work as a missionary or take over a parish where another of God's servants had passed away.

No blood stained his cheeks, wet or dry. Whatever he had done at the ranch house after stabbing Annette, he must have kept his distance from Saber. And again here, at Slim's Respite.

Where the hell had Saber gone?

"A beer, of whatsoever you've served last," Balthazar said, wedging between two barstools. Coins clinked on the bar.

Slim looked to the shuttered entrance and then went to work. His trembling hands spilled froth down the glass mug's side, and they trembled harder as he wiped it up and passed the drink to Balthazar.

Annette didn't want a fight here, and Slim and Arch were in no shape to win one. Saber might have taken her scraping blade with her to finish Mortimer like she'd finished Frank, but her taint lingered in Slim's Respite. She had shaken the men. If Balthazar slashed his dagger at their hearts, they might not be as lucky as Annette. She certainly wouldn't get lucky twice if he came at her again.

Arch wandered between the tables, a lost captain traveling some wooden archipelago. "How'd you make it?"

Balthazar grasped his mug and raised it. "Clouds hide stars and moon, so I imagine your lit windows would draw any traveler." A stiffness took his voice at those last two words.

"But how'd you make it past the demon?" Arch asked.

Balthazar turned with a cool stare and sipped his drink. Foam dappled his lower lip. "You've seen strangers tonight?"

Arch couldn't give him another word. His bowed legs rocked with an absent sea as it swept him back to the table islands.

Slim leaned over the bar. "Not sure."

"Not sure?" Balthazar turned to Slim again. "Have you told your lawmen?"

"The sheriff passed recently." Slim glanced over Balthazar's shoulder as if searching the saloon for Annette and not finding her. "We're between laws at the moment."

"Surely not between God's laws. Your town must have a minister."

"Out and about," Slim said. "And it's not much of a night for travelers."

"That is so," Balthazar said, almost cheerful. "Yet we travel when we must search."

He lifted the glass to his lips again and drank deeply. Annette hadn't heard any horse outside the ranch, nothing to say Balthazar had come riding in. He must have walked to the Klein ranch from parts unknown and then followed the southbound road to Low's Bend, the same as Saber. Thirsty traveling, even on a cool night.

Arch banged his hip into a table, clacking its legs against the floor. "Lord be with us," he said, his voice a soft, feathery rustle as he hugged his chest.

Balthazar began to turn, and Annette slid deeper behind the piano, only the side of one eye peeking out. There was something spidery about his movements in the light, as if his shadow cast thin legs to prod every surface and see more than his eyes might. He knew the saloon didn't make sense tonight, but he hadn't figured out why.

"Arch lost a good friend," Slim said. Disbelief haunted his voice.

Balthazar's arm—deliberate, purposeful—drew Arch close to the bar. "Tell me your name, child of God."

Arch swallowed hard. "Archibald Bower."

"Rest easy, Archibald." Balthazar squeezed Arch's shoulder. "If you are with the Lord, then the Lord is with you. The same is so for your late friend and our good barkeep."

Arch nodded, shaking, and then pulled his handkerchief from his back pocket and wiped it down his face.

Slim leaned to one side and spotted Annette. He mouthed something she couldn't figure out, and she didn't know how to tell him why she was hiding without alerting Balthazar. To tell would catch Slim off-guard, while Balthazar was already poised to fight and kill.

Neither Slim nor Arch understood. Saber had put a fear in them, and Balthazar offered the hard-boned reliance of God and the general comfort men fell into over each other's company.

Balthazar clapped Arch's arms. "I think I've found a little of what I'm searching for tonight. Godliness in the realm of good men." He turned toward the corner, and Annette ducked out of sight. "Come, this place needs heavenly reverence and joy. Do not despair, for the Lord makes Himself known in each small piece of us."

His boots thudded nearer, nearer, and a slow hum slid up his throat. He paused on the far side of the piano. Annette wound her limbs around her torso and crammed herself small into the corner. One hand covered her mouth against a shrill gasp.

"A fine instrument," Balthazar said. Four rising notes thrummed through the piano. He paused and then tapped out four more. "Anyone mind?"

Annette heard no answer, but Slim or Arch must have nodded or shaken their heads. A wooden scrape chased the piano's stool from beneath its keyboard, and then a Saber-like wooden groan ripped through the floor as Balthazar sat down. He gave the piano keys another four testing notes.

He had to know she sat two feet ahead of him, behind wood and wire and whatever else made up a piano's innards. He was playing with her, seeing how tense he could pull her nerves until she snapped, right? Had to be.

But either way, if she scurried off while he busied himself, he might lose track of her. Music would draw Sylvia and Treasure out of the upstairs rooms again. They would notice her sneaking. They would help.

Curious tinkling notes folded into a slow, somber tune. Balthazar played it twice, warming up his fingers and wrists. The piano went tinny at a couple of notes, but he played like he didn't hear the difference.

And then he began to sing.

Joseph was an old man, and an old man was he,
When he married Mary, the Queen of Galilee.

The piano hummed through the floor, and each chord trembled in Annette's teeth.

When Joseph was married, and Mary home had brought,
Mary proved with child, and Joseph knew it not.

"A little off-tune," Arch said, suddenly close. The piano must have masked his approaching footsteps. He sniffled and then said, "A tweak should fix it. Here."

He appeared halfway into Annette's view. Both hands flattened over the piano lid and gave a hard shove. A strumming rattle echoed through its firm body and sent Annette skittering until she crouched flat against the wall. Balthazar went on playing.

Joseph and Mary walked through a garden gay,
Where the cherries, they grew upon every tree.

Annette caught sight of the black hat around the piano's corner as Balthazar glanced at Arch. Each raised their heads to nod, an agreement that the piano sounded sharper and right, and Annette scuttled along the wall until she huddled beneath the nearest round table. The saloon stretched desert-wide from here to the staircase.

Balthazar peered around behind the piano. Only flailing dust motes might give Annette away; she'd left nothing else. He settled at a lethargic pace, and his hands found the tune again, not so tinny anymore.

O then bespoke Mary, with words both meek and mild,

CRUEL ANGELS PAST SUNDOWN

'O gather me cherries, Joseph, for I am with child.'
Annette pressed her fingers to the floor and slinked between the table undersides.

And then replied Joseph, with anger was he,
'Let the father of this child gather cherries for thee.'
Annette's dress bunched at her ankles. She wondered if Balthazar might not recognize her indoors and mistake her for some other blood-drenched woman. She doubted it.

A frail voice cried in the distance. Likely a coyote, but maybe not. Saber stalked Low's Bend, and she might have finally finished off Mortimer. The cry stirred a heat inside Annette and coiled piano wire-taut around her spine. Her arms and legs stiffened as heavy hands pounded the piano keys with righteous intent.

O then bespoke our Savior, all in His mother's womb:
'Bow down, good cherry tree, to my mother's hand.'
Balthazar's muscles corded around his back and limbs, black jacket stretching, every part of him keying into the piano and joining its heaviest notes with his full-throated song. The outside cry drowned in singing, breaking its hold on Annette and letting her slip to another table's underside. Soon she would reach the corner table and then creep up the stairs along the wall, with the banister to hide her from Balthazar. Sylvia and Treasure had to be standing at the railing above already, watching him play.

The uppermost sprig bowed down to Mary's knee:
'Thus you may see, Joseph, these cherries are for me.'
Slim had to be watching Annette by now, confused but silent. Arch, too. She couldn't glance their way for help, or above at Sylvia and Treasure who might understand better, not even back to Balthazar to be certain he didn't watch out the corner of his eye.

'O eat your cherries, Mary, O eat your cherries now;
O eat your cherries, Mary, that grow upon the bough.'
The floor scraped beneath Annette's hands and boots as she passed the front door, to the corner table, into its

shadow. One more push, up the steps. She crept toward the lowest and glanced up. Sylvia and Treasure had returned to the railing. Their puzzled faces watched Annette. She would explain when she reached them.

As Joseph was a walking, he heard an angel sing:
'This night shall be born our heavenly—'

Annette leaned to climb toward them, her lips begging for help.

Piano keys shouted a cacophonous note, their music clanging so hard to a stop that Annette's head whipped to one side, to the saloon.

To Balthazar. "—king." His gaze chilled from the shadow of his black hat.

Annette urged one leg forward, but she was bent up, a bad posture for hurrying, and every muscle froze in place.

Balthazar no longer seemed a man of ordinary height. He towered again as he stood from the stool, even with the whole saloon stretching between the piano and the corner table, and his shadow reached for Annette.

"I should have made certain," he said. "I meant no pain. Only ending." He took a firm step and slid one hand into his coat. "Only mercy and release."

Treasure clutched the railing; Sylvia stood resolute beside her. They weren't part of this yet and could still hide in their rooms. Annette didn't know how to tell them they would lose their chance if they helped her.

Same for the men. Arch stood frozen at the piano. His mouth hung slack as he turned toward the bar, where Slim stared back, his jaw set. They both looked from Balthazar to Annette, studying his gait, her hand creeping up her still-bloody dress, the shrinking space between them. They were realizing too late to stop this.

Balthazar's hand withdrew from his jacket, and the crucifix-dagger gleamed in the meek candlelight.

SEVEN:
WRATH

ANNETTE CRAWLED TO standing against the staircase banister. She shouldn't have been here. She should have been hiding behind the bar, but Arch had let Balthazar storm inside like God had laid claim to Slim's property.

Balthazar passed the shuttered front door, his mouth set in a mean line.

A hand grasped his sleeve. "Hang on then," Arch said. His forehead furrowed at the dagger in Balthazar's hand. "You let her be. Thought you said you wanted godliness in the realm of good men."

One floorboard groaned beneath Balthazar's heavy step. He would stop now to deliver a sermon, like he had given outside the ranch house. Explaining his work meant more than singing and reassuring. The rambling would last long enough for Annette to slip away. She wasn't so drowsy with Saber's red nightmare that she would stand and listen this time. She could escape before the crucifix-dagger cut through her heart.

Balthazar glanced at Arch's hand. "Submit yourselves therefore to God," he said. A shine took over his eyes and then faded beneath his hat's shadow as if someone had lit and doused a lantern in his skull. "Resist the devil, and he will flee from you."

Annette had to have imagined the glow; people's eyes

didn't do that. Some trick of the light, an odd reflection, the way a glass might catch sunshine through a window to cast a lit circle onto some nearby wall.

Fingers slid from Balthazar's sleeve as Arch dropped his arm. His face fell into slack-jawed terror, more broken than he'd looked when Saber had shoved at the saloon doors. If she still prowled out there, he would meet her soon—he tore from Balthazar's arm to the entrance, tossed up the bracing plank, and yanked one shutter aside. Panic sent him dashing through the doorway. One swinging saloon door batted the air behind him. If he feared the crucifix-dagger, he wouldn't find better with Saber's blade out there, but he didn't know that.

He was already gone. Balthazar had sent him away.

Annette wouldn't get the same treatment. She leaned toward the wooden steps. One foot at a time, get to the top, hide in one of the rooms, and lock the door.

Except Balthazar could kick in those doors, and as Sylvia had said, the upstairs would become a trap. Annette slid around the floor side of the banister. Balthazar weaved step by step, changing course to match hers.

"There ain't a reason for this," she said, stumbling backward from him.

"A blessing in one is a sickness in another, and I will cut it out," Balthazar said.

"I ain't sick. You cut me before, but I stitched it up. There's no sheriff here anymore, no marshal." None of this was coming out right. That furnace inside Annette wanted her to sound powerful, but her voice came shaky as her limbs. "The one bounty hunter who passes through won't bother you if there's no bounty. No one's coming if you let me go. No one has to know. No one hunts you."

"I fear no men." Balthazar had stolen any strength of voice, his tone telling the air itself to bend and obey like the cherry tree in his song. Some holy wind blew at his back. "God knows my heart. But I'm truly sorry, Annette

Ruthie Klein." His crucifix-dagger smiled in the light. "Heaven awaits."

A heavy metal clack froze Balthazar in place. His head remained fixed on Annette, but his eyes trailed to one side.

Slim approached from her left, arm slung around his shotgun's wooden comb, its barrels aiming two black eyes at Balthazar and digging through his soul.

Pull the trigger, Annette wanted to say, but her throat only croaked. *End this*.

Balthazar offered Slim a too-warm smile. "I have no firearm, young man." His voice had slipped from stern to friendly, but it seemed no less powerful. "Only that with which the Lord arms me."

Slim said nothing. Another cautious step, another.

Annette eyed Balthazar's hands. "He has the—the!" Her words were gone again. Saber's fault.

"The Lord makes firm the steps of the one who delights in him," Balthazar said, friendliness gone.

A thousand fireflies flickered bright in his throat and then died as he twisted toward Slim. Every motion came graceful and deliberate, and Annette would have been envious had his blade not glimmered in her eye again.

"The dagger!" she finally shouted.

Too late. The crucifix-dagger slung from Balthazar's hand and buried into Slim's thigh as Slim pulled the trigger. The shot blasted at the ceiling, spraying splinters across Balthazar as he charged. One arm batted the shotgun away and sent it swirling across the floor, where it struck a table leg.

Balthazar grabbed Slim up by the collar in both hands and slammed him onto another table. It crashed beneath Slim's back, landing him in a pile of shattered wood. Balthazar then gripped the dagger by its Christly hilt and ripped it free.

Slim howled in pain and skittered backward on both hands and one leg alongside the bar. A thin red trail snaked after him across the floorboards.

Sylvia or Treasure gasped above. They hadn't retreated, but neither of them could be of much help. The saloon's comforting odors sank beneath a coppery stench.

Annette eyed the shotgun.

"Tell me your name, child of God," Balthazar said, storming over Slim's blood trail.

Slim's back struck the far wall. Nowhere left to crawl. He turned hard eyes up at Balthazar.

"Slim," he said, chest heaving.

"No, not your alias." Balthazar's shadow twisted beneath the chandelier. "You gave that name to yourself, born of a lying tongue, not given through your parents by the Lord, but adopted. What is your Christian name?"

Slim patted the wall, the floor, as if making certain he wasn't dreaming. Annette slinked behind Balthazar, her steps ginger across treacherous floorboards.

"It's verbal dressing by infernal means," Balthazar said. "Do you understand? You hold sin on your tongue. No alias, no nickname." His knee bent, and he aimed the crucifix-dagger at Slim's face. "I would cut these guises off, and free your Christian name for the tongue of the Almighty."

Annette knelt too, beside the table. The shotgun's iron warmed her fingertips. Out of the corner of her eye, Slim mouthed, *Hide*, but she couldn't. Her fingers closed around the gun and lifted.

"Forgive me," Balthazar said. "I meant no suffering. I'm yet unpracticed in taking lives in the name of Christ, but my work is almost ended. Soon, I will nurture, once I've finished with you. And then—" His head turned over one shoulder. "—with you."

Annette braced the shotgun's butt to her collar and stood, one forefinger rattling over the trigger. "Drop the dagger."

Balthazar climbed from Slim and again stretched too tall for the world. One unworried eye slid down the length of the barrels.

"Lower it," he said. Perfect stillness, perfect control.

Annette's hands trembled. She only had one shot. She pressed the butt harder against her, and a sharp pain jabbed through her chest as if Balthazar had slung the dagger through her breast again. Her wound would open under pressure. She might falter, and then he really would stab her a second time.

Balthazar opened his mouth again. The light caught in his eyes, the same as Annette had seen when he frightened Arch away, in his throat when he tossed the dagger into Slim. Some magic stirred in Balthazar, the kind Annette didn't believe, but she trusted her eyes.

And pulled the trigger.

The shotgun kicked a cry up her throat and fired into the wooden wall. No blood in the scar—she'd missed Balthazar entirely. She cracked open the barrels and stock to pull out the steaming rounds, but where did Slim keep his fresh slugs?

"You are pregnant with sin, but you wish to be holy," Balthazar said. "And holy love cannot slay me."

He hadn't finished with Slim yet, but Annette overtook his world. He was a man who could be lured and distracted, but that would only save her life if she could keep him switching between targets forever.

Gunsmoke rippled up the shotgun. Annette squeezed its wood and iron, letting the heat stir through her skin. That furnace sensation billowed in her chest, and her teeth gritted at thoughts of these empty barrels, her dead husband, the night that wouldn't end, and how Balthazar wouldn't stop coming.

"Hell with your holy love!" she shrieked.

Balthazar tilted his head, and the shadow cast by his hat darkened his face.

Annette clacked the shotgun shut, clutched its barrels in both hands, and raised it over her shoulder. "Hell with your preaching." She swung the makeshift cudgel down and slammed the wooden comb against Balthazar's arm.

"And your moralizing." Another swing and the wood cracked against his shoulder. A tremor quaked up the shotgun and through her arm, but she pushed through and swung a third time. "And fuck you, and the horse you rode in on. Unless you're telling me why my husband's dead, shut your goddamn mouth."

Balthazar snapped his dagger forward. "He was a soul by the wayside."

"I know that!" Annette darted out of the blade's way and clubbed Balthazar's side. Flames danced inside her, and she danced with them. This anger was unfamiliar but delicious, as if Balthazar had thrown open a forbidden furnace door inside her and unleashed tempting hellfire. "My Frank was a good man. He took in my late mother and brother, loved me no matter what I did, drank down every word like a man dying of thirst."

"And now he has finished dying." Balthazar reached out to steady her. He would drive the dagger where he'd driven it before, this time all the way to her heart. Finish what he started. "He is dead."

Annette smashed the shotgun against Balthazar's forearm. Bone cracked with a sick wetness. He grunted and lunged, and she cracked the comb against his bicep. His fingers twitched, loosening around the crucifix-dagger's wooden grip.

"And there is a wrath in you," he said.

Annette screamed into another swing. She stopped making sense, making words. Her tongue grew fat at the back of her throat, and every spitting sound flew in curses and shrieks and seeing red. Not the drowsy nightmare, but a crimson curtain across her eyes, thumping and alive with blood vessels and throbbing muscle. She wanted to rend Balthazar open. She needed to see him pour dark red across the saloon floor.

Her legs tensed, and she made for another wild pounce, dagger be damned. She didn't care if he stabbed her heart and sliced it in two; to crack his skull open would make hers a life well lived. They both lunged.

CRUEL ANGELS PAST SUNDOWN

A familiar two-note whistle shut Annette's furnace door, and her furious lunge broke into an awkward stagger.

Balthazar kept his control. His dagger sliced toward her chest.

The room tilted in a blur of dust and gunfire. One round blasted into Balthazar's side and sent him stumbling. Another round chewed into his ribcage.

Annette ducked toward the saloon tables as he tore past her and crashed where the stairs climbed toward the second floor. She froze in place and waited for him to turn again with a light in his eyes, an unstoppable need.

But his precise control was gone. He slumped beneath the stairway banister, and his crucifix-dagger clattered to the floor. Annette wheeled toward the entrance.

And saw her.

EIGHT:
GLORIA

WHITE TEETH SHINED in a deep umber face. A wide-brimmed tan hat perched above her head of short curls. She wore denim and a loose shirt around her broad frame, and the swinging saloon door pressed against her tawny duster. One fist clutched a lean iron pistol, aimed across the room, with her other hand raised flat above its hammer.

She should have been too grandiose and beautiful for this world, and yet here she stood in the lowly half-shuttered doorway of Slim's Respite, a long way from the desert and longer still from England. A wind-whipped ragged tail of torn coat behind her seemed to pause in a mid-flight moment of stillness, more an oil painting than real, but she had breath and a heartbeat, and Annette couldn't have asked for more. Just these elements to have her here.

Gloria Travers.

She kept her pistol trained below the stairway banister, but Balthazar was little more than a groaning lump. Her flat hand crawled from the hammer, and her other hand cautiously slid the pistol into its holster. She eased her stance with a sigh.

All the rage melted down Annette's throat. "Gloria!" she shouted. She flew across the saloon and crashed into Gloria's chest, fawning at her duster, shirt, cheeks, seeking old scars for familiarity and new cuts to tend. "Are you hurt?"

"Not that I'm aware, Butterfly," Gloria said, and the curl in her voice suggested an ocean had parted to let her reach Low's Bend tonight.

Sylvia and Treasure skirted down the stairs, calling relieved greetings as they came.

Annette couldn't let Gloria through to them, to anyone. She clutched tight, and the shotgun loosened from her fingers.

Gloria caught it and called over Annette's shoulder. "Slim, you can't hand these to the untrained. They're dangerous, don't you see?" She nudged Annette back enough to set the shotgun on a still-standing table and then took Annette's chin in one hand. "There now, Butterfly, what have you fluttered your way into this time?"

I let Frank die, Annette started to say. The words sputtered on her lips.

Gloria chinned past Annette's shoulder at Balthazar. "A rough one, I see. Someone owe him money, that it?" She looked around the saloon. "One of you lot?"

"You should've seen her, Gloria," Treasure said, giving Balthazar a wide berth. "Nettie wouldn't run, wouldn't hide. She took at that man like a wild animal, beating and clobbering. Never seen the like before." She glanced behind, where Sylvia stared at something on the floor and followed a red snaking puddle toward Slim, who slumped by the far wall. "Damn, Slim, you're a wreck."

He coughed out an answer, but Annette missed it.

Gloria held her chin tight, their gazes locked. Her face was hard. "Don't go brawling with dangerous men. If you've a death wish, tell me."

Annette wanted to shake her head, but her face was stuck in Gloria's grip.

"Are you happy to see me, or have you finally had enough?" Gloria asked. Her hand slid from Annette's face to her blood-darkened dress. "Don't kiss me and break my heart. You make it hard to leave, but don't make it hurt to come back."

Annette eased into Gloria's arms. She had no idea what had come over her when she went tearing into Balthazar. The night was heavy, and she'd had enough.

"I'm sorry," she said.

Gloria looked Annette over, and her expression softened. "It's all well, I suppose. We'll make a hunter of you yet, my bricky girl."

Better they had made Annette a hunter sooner. She would have fought through the drowsiness at the ranch and battled Saber off Frank's chest, out of their bed.

"My husband's dead," Annette said, her tongue dry, her eyes wet. She didn't have the heart to say his name aloud right now. "Murdered."

"Oh, Butterfly." Gloria held her again. There was a quake in her voice Annette couldn't read.

"He was a good man."

"I know he was."

"I don't know what—" A shudder cut Annette off, and she sank deeper into Gloria's arms.

Some conversation needed having, but this awful night still swirled around them, beginning with that bone woman and her sword and a dead body on a bed. Frank had given his blessing to Annette's divided heart. He had loved her and followed her everywhere she went, to strange places and flower-scented rooms, and when she told him he couldn't follow to Gloria, he had only kissed Annette's forehead, and then her lips, and wished her well.

He was gone, and what did that mean for her? For Gloria?

When Annette leaned back, she found no answers in Gloria's face. She squeezed Gloria's hand and almost made to kiss her here as if to coax thoughts through those lips.

But Gloria tilted her head toward Balthazar. "And him?" she asked. "He's the one that killed Frank?"

Balthazar grasped his side with one hand; the other

dangled beside him. Two bullet holes tore open his jacket, and blood spread in damp rings. If he lifted it, Annette expected she'd see a red sunrise stain the once-white shirt beneath. She might have hurt his arm with the swinging shotgun. He deserved worse. So did Saber.

"Not him," Annette said.

There was more to it, but she couldn't find the words. Trying to explain why tonight's evil had bared its teeth would mean having anything to tell. She had been accosted by one demon in the skin of a pregnant woman, and the other in the skin of a minister, both toothed with steel. Blood coated their hands and hearts, but why had tonight happened? Why the anguish and death?

Sylvia's voice cut through the questions. "Slim needs help."

Treasure crouched beside Slim, and her petticoat flared. "He's ripped up pretty good," she said.

"I'll find Dr. Hastings, loves," Gloria said, backing toward the door. "A moment or less."

"No one's seen him," Slim said. "A week. Could be the demon got him, I don't know."

He grunted some Spanish curse Annette didn't recognize and waved a hand, a gesture she couldn't read either. Blood slithered between his fingers. Were Gloria to ride off for another town and bring a doctor here, Slim wouldn't be waiting when they returned.

"Get me that needle again," Annette said. "And thread."

Treasure shot up from Slim, her face wide. "Oh." She darted past Sylvia, Annette, and Gloria, and hurried upstairs. "Oh," she said again.

Annette crept toward Slim. "And something to cut his pants."

"They're cut enough, don't you think?" Slim said.

Annette had almost reached him when Sylvia's hand latched around her forearm. She flashed a severe gaze.

"What about the other man?" Sylvia whispered.

"He won't live long enough to tell anyone what he sees," Annette whispered back, but she bent in front of Slim so she could help him while blocking Balthazar's view.

Sylvia returned to staring at the blood trail. The boarding room women never cleaned the floor; Slim hired a local kid to do that, and he'd already gone home before Annette's arrival. This would not be the first time someone mopped up one night's blood the next morning.

Gloria paced with heavy footsteps between the blood trail and crumpled Balthazar. He hadn't moved since his collapse against the staircase. She kicked gently at one of his boots.

"Got anything to say for yourself?" she asked.

Balthazar glanced up at her and then down at his hands in fits and starts. His teeth chattered.

"Cat's got your tongue, eh?" Gloria nudged again. "Black British bounty hunters don't much frequent your bloody parish, preacher? Nor do we gun you down often. I'd wager you've never been shot before, is that right?"

"Pride is unbecoming," Balthazar said, his words steady. Blood pooled down his jacket, and still strength swelled in his voice. "You have struck down a servant of the Lord."

"I can see that. Interesting interpretation for godliness, if you don't mind my saying."

"You do not know godliness. In staying Abraham's blade from Isaac, the Lord told His servants He will no longer demand blood sacrifice." Balthazar eyed the crucifix-dagger at his feet as if it lay a hundred miles away. "He will nonetheless accept them."

"Is that right?" Gloria tapped her pistol's grip, jutting from its holster on her right hip. "Looks to me like you'll have a chance to clarify that with the Lord soon enough."

Treasure pounded down the steps and returned to Annette and Slim. She clutched the same needle and thread she'd given Annette to stitch her skin shut. Good enough for her, good enough for Slim. Treasure also held a musty cream-colored scarf as a soon-to-be bandage. She huddled beside them, helping to give Slim privacy at least from Balthazar.

Not that it seemed to matter. His eyes were only for Gloria and himself.

"He ain't dying, right?" Treasure asked, her voice cracking. She grasped Slim's fingers in one gloved hand.

"Everyone dies," Sylvia said, toneless.

Annette took the needle and thread and then chinned at Slim's waist. "Help unbuckle his belt. Yes, like that."

The wound was ragged; the crucifix-dagger might have skirted along the bone. Annette couldn't guess the damage inside, could only do her best to stymie the blood from slobbering out. She bent over Slim's thigh, pinched the flesh shut, and told Treasure to keep holding his hand. Between his legs and curly hair, Slim didn't much resemble Frank below the waist. Darker, and softer, and in the rare moments anyone had a chance to notice, Slim had said he kept the pieces inside him, or had them kicked off by a mule, or whatever excuse dismissed a raised eyebrow or intrusive questioner.

But between Slim, Annette, and the boarding room ladies, they kept each other's secrets. Gloria, too. Maybe there were others Annette had never met, a whole community of traveling secret-keepers. Slim's Respite might have offered them a mutual crossroads, an unknown reason Annette felt safe to follow Treasure up those stairs the first time, and all that had come after, and everything with Gloria.

And now Annette had to shove a needle through his skin. He didn't deserve this any better than Frank, but tonight didn't seem to care what anyone deserved. She tried not to glance at Slim's face, gritted with pain.

Gloria gestured at the bar. "Pour that on to clean it first. Rough means, but it will do the trick."

Sylvia plucked the whiskey bottle down and tilted it toward Slim's leg. Her uncertain gaze fixed on the seeping wound.

"This'll hurt," Annette said, raising her needle. "And this, too."

"Other men have had worse." Slim grasped the bottle's neck and swallowed two harsh gulps. It spilled down his hairless chin and neck and dampened his shirt. He squeezed the back of his head against the wall and pressed the bottle into Sylvia's hands. "I can take it."

He hissed as Sylvia poured a splash of whiskey across his torn thigh, and then he stifled a groan when Annette jammed the needle into his damp skin. The sinew around the wound was frayed and raw, and she had to weave through thick sections or else the thread might tear from the meat, but to stitch someone else was easier than stitching herself. Blood caked her fingernails. She was getting used to that.

Gloria paced harder on the far side of the room. "Anyone care to tell me who the devil our new ministerial friend might be?"

Treasure looked away from Slim. "He jabbed Nettie at her ranch, must've followed her here, jabbed Slim, too. Likes to jab folk, that's who *he* is. Probably jabbed a preacher to get his coat."

The thread dampened around Slim's wound, but its open mouth closed bit by bit. Soon it would form a similar grimace to Annette's breast. She hoped Dr. Hastings would come back sometime soon, certain to treat Slim better, but with strangers like Saber and Balthazar wandering around, Slim might've had a point—the only doctor in Low's Bend could be dead.

Balthazar's throat rumbled wetly. "I am a man of God," he said. "I have dwelled in His light, passed on His word in churches, on streets. And for this, the Lord has vested in me a holy burden beyond your understanding and comprehension. There is more work to do in this world than spread the word."

"Rather, bothering the good people of Low's Bend?" Gloria asked.

Balthazar almost growled. "Only for her sake."

Annette kept to her needle, thread, and Slim's flesh. In, out, and through, as if Balthazar couldn't see her, couldn't speak to her.

"Let her live, and you'll regret it," he went on. "She suffers traces of the pale mark, and she'll echo it here. By the end, she'll lose her speech and walk an endless dream, and any near her will walk it too, for fear of laying a hand upon her."

Annette paused. An endless dream, or a nightmare? "That demon," she said. "She came to the ranch. To me."

"And you tried to help her," Balthazar said. His words sounded damp and coated in blood. "Even so changed, she is beautiful."

Gloria clicked her tongue. "Men always dream up spirits and demons as beautiful women. They know nothing of real ghosts." She looked longingly toward the bar, as if someone stood there watching her.

"There are no ghosts but the Holy Spirit." Balthazar seemed to straighten. "And there is the watchful power of the one Lord. The world beyond our sight is one of angels. Heaven awaits, and miracles walk the Earth." He turned again to Annette. "Sometimes we must chase their consequences."

The saloon grew still with a floorboard's creak. Annette wanted Gloria to have taken another step, but she hadn't moved, hands on her hips. There was no reason she'd notice the noise; no one had said a word to her yet about Saber.

Sylvia waved an arm in Annette's face. "Don't stop now. Save Slim."

Annette's hands remained still. She listened for footsteps, a rising gale, some further element of Mortimer's predicted storm before a hand of ash and bone had dragged him into the night, but she only heard another long wooden groan.

Slim jerked his head from the wall. "It's back. Gloria, girls—the shutters."

Gloria scowled over the saloon, her lips pursed. She didn't understand. She had only got into town minutes ago, and she couldn't know every hell that had come to Low's Bend.

Balthazar leaned his head beneath the stairway banister. "And I suppose I'm here chasing *her*, too. For a different purpose, another responsibility."

Annette swallowed hard. "Why?" she asked, fixing her hatred on those too-blue eyes.

"Because she carries my grandson," Balthazar said, his face filling with pride. "And He is the Lord."

NINE:
THE RIGHTEOUS HAND

ANNETTE NEEDED TO finish stitching Slim's leg, and quick, but Balthazar had thrown too many new thoughts into her head. Never mind that most of it had to be bullshit. She couldn't picture Saber as a daughter, not even to a monster like him. Not as a mother either, to God or anyone else, despite her round belly.

"What are you on about?" Gloria asked, half-laughing. "Carries the Lord. Listen to yourself."

"Your mockery belies your lack of faith," Balthazar said. "It is small against the truth."

The creaky-house groan wove through the saloon walls. They seemed surrounded by Saber, as if she'd stretched through the night into a snake coiling around Slim's Respite. Likely she had the same blank look on her face, maybe bloodied now for having dipped that overlong tongue into Mortimer's insides.

Gloria started for the half-shuttered doorway. "I'll have a look."

"You can't!" Annette cried.

Treasure nodded beside her. "You should've heard Nettie's story. Block up that door, and don't tangle with it. Damn thing murdered Frank."

"Now look, I'm in no habit to play the damsel, loves," Gloria said. "I'm back from hunting down the damn Chesterton Brothers. Remember those three? Each was a far cry meaner than one little preacher and his girl." She pivoted again to the saloon door. "Anyone care to join me?"

Sylvia broke from Slim's side. "I'll find a lantern."

Annette's fingertips pinched around the warm needle and pushed it through Slim's skin. She thought of Balthazar's crucifix-dagger across her chest and his daughter's blade in a bed back at the ranch house.

"Be careful," Annette said. "She has a cavalry saber. And around her, it's hard to think straight."

Sylvia found a lantern behind the bar and lit it with a match. The glow held soft against her eyepatch.

"She means it, Gloria," Slim said, still clenching his teeth at Annette's needlework. "Your eyes run red when she's close. No seas tonto, and shutter that door."

"I've faced worse than a pregnant woman with a sword." Gloria scowled between Annette, Treasure, and Slim. "What's the matter with you all? I'm supposed to ride in for drinks and company, not a saloon full of cowards. " She sighed, and the wind seemed to sigh with her. "Honestly, you three."

Annette pushed the needle, and pulled, in and out. Nearly finished. Gloria was headed out the door, and there would be Saber, emaciated yet full-bellied, naked as a new tooth freed of its gum, and her blade waiting. A pale mark, Balthazar had said, and he bore a duty handed to him from on high. There would be no faith in the company of this man.

Annette pulled the thread taut, knotted it, and broke it with her teeth. "It'll be alright," she said, taking the cream scarf from Treasure and binding Slim's thigh in a makeshift bandage. Annette then stood and faced the staircase. "Your daughter, Balthazar. What'd you do to her?"

The question froze Gloria as she placed one hand on the shutter-free saloon door. Sylvia slipped back, still holding the lit lantern. They both glanced at Annette and then at Balthazar.

Pink drool bubbled down the side of his mouth. "I blessed her, nothing else."

Annette watched and waited, her arms tensing. Fire clawed up her throat. Her needle wanted to drive through his eye, deep into the brain.

"If God would not answer her prayers, she would call another power," Balthazar said. "She had already gone for help of the flesh. I couldn't allow this blasphemy, too. Instead, I called to God, and He laid His curse upon her through holy messengers to protect both mother and child."

"Your head is cooked, my friend," Slim said. He tugged his pants back up his waist, his thigh damp with blood and liquor. "Been living in the desert too long."

Annette wanted to tell about the light in Balthazar's face, but she clapped her jaw shut. What had she really seen?

"Slim has the right of it," Gloria said, strolling back to Balthazar. "All the people who've suffered across the centuries, through all the world and all time, prayers only answered in the vaguest ways, but you—you are the man God answers."

"Your words exactly," Balthazar said. Redness had overtaken the lower half of his shirt. "How is God to find the chosen among the suffering when so many people suffer? Their toil gives them no merit. Faith is rarer, and that is how God chooses. If He finds me His most pious servant, I'm not the man who'll question that judgment. His messengers speak His will." He turned cold eyes to Annette. He had looked at her too many times tonight. "The Lord's kindness is spent, and I'll see that none follow in my daughter's sin."

Muscles corded up Annette's spine. "But she followed me. Came to my home. Why?"

"Hell is a lonely place." Any mirth faded from Balthazar's face, and he winced in pain. "She can't escape her loneliness, but she can drag others into her burden. I expect that's why she set upon you, and why I found your husband's innards cut from his chest and gut. Suffer as she suffers."

Annette was ready to dash across the saloon and claw Balthazar's face into red ribbons. This fury was strange. She'd assumed he had opened this furnace door inside her, but maybe Saber was to blame, somehow planting a fire inside Annette before cutting Frank open to pull his pieces out.

Slim's boots scuffed the floor, and Annette helped him to his feet. Gloria paced from Balthazar toward Annette, Treasure, and Slim. Sylvia followed, still clutching the lantern.

"He wasn't the first," Balthazar went on. "Neither are you. The sickness takes root, and there's little time to cut it down before you become something almost like my daughter, but without purpose, for there will be no immaculate conception as there is with her."

Balthazar had to be bleeding so badly that he was getting drowsy, talking nonsense. Saber's pregnancy was no immaculate conception. He didn't know the father, that was it.

"That woman out there," Slim said, his voice hoarse. "Got a kid in her?"

"Ready to come out by the looks of her," Annette said. "But I don't know how far along for sure."

Slim chinned across the saloon. "Bet our preacher does. Here this bloodthirsty chachalaca rides in on his high horse from places of desolation, the kind where someone might not notice people out of place, might not ask questions." He looked across sullen faces, each mouth set in a line. "Come on, we're all thinking it. Immaculate conception, he says, y una mierda. We know what he did to his daughter." One hand reached for the bar's ashtray, where the last remnants of a cigar smoldered. Slim stuffed the end into his mouth and puffed a blue trail. "Getting put up with a child we didn't want?" He lowered his voice. "It could happen to any of us here, except him."

Another creaking groan slid down Annette's spine. Saber acting like this, looking like this—easy to see as sunrise that Slim was right.

"I committed no sin upon my daughter," Balthazar said, and again added, "I blessed her."

"You think you're quite something," Gloria said. Her fingers drummed her holster.

"There were consequences to the Lord's attention, but this has always been so. Exodus. Job. The archangel Gabriel promises there is nothing to fear, for my daughter is the blessed mother of God."

Another groan tore Gloria's gaze to the back door beyond the bar, and then she veered on Balthazar. "Christ's mother spoke like that?"

The next moan sounded distant. Saber was wandering off again. She hadn't tried the front door this time, perhaps too lost in her own red nightmare. Annette hadn't started seeing it until after she blacked out at the ranch house, that dream world of organs and bones. If some sickness had passed from Saber to Annette, this might be a symptom, the way a harsh fever brought on strange visions.

Slim stumbled toward the entrance and eyed the shutter Arch had tossed aside. "We can't stay here forever," he said. "Of course, she can't stay out there forever. Which of us waits out the other?"

Annette pointed to Slim's leg. "Careful, or it'll bust open."

"Can't have that. But we can't stay, either." Slim hobbled from the entrance. An insistent draft followed him, swinging one saloon door free and banging the other against its shutter. He reeked of whiskey. "You managing?"

"He got you worse than he got me," Annette said.

Slim aimed his cigar from her chest wound to his leg. "I won't tell if you won't."

"Yes, sir." Annette gave an exaggerated nod and a bigger smile. For a brief moment, she thought the night might turn for the better. Or at least it wouldn't get any worse now that Gloria was here.

But beneath the low wind, she caught Balthazar muttering to himself. Garbled syllables rained in red spit and twisting lips.

"What's he doing?" Treasure asked. She seemed poised to get close, tend to him.

Sylvia nudged her back toward the bar. "Praying," she said.

Annette glanced at her hands. Doubtful she could stitch Balthazar's bullet wounds, and the bullets would still sit inside and poison him. He didn't deserve help or pity, but a sinking in her heart didn't want him to sit there, knowing he was going to die, begging for help that wouldn't come.

And yet she wanted to tear his face open.

Balthazar stroked one finger over his coat where the black fabric oozed red ringlets, an almost confused look on his face, and then he shut his eyes. "Forgive me, I do not understand."

His head thrust back as if someone behind him had grasped his hair and yanked hard, but no one stood at the stairway banister. Every part of him stiffened, his body pulled as taut as piano wire. He jerked as if Arch had come and slammed his lid, but no one touched him, not that Annette could see.

"Yes, I'm listening!" Balthazar shouted, desperate now. "And I am not afraid!"

Gloria glanced at Annette and then the others. They echoed her blank face. The saloon dimmed slightly as if a chandelier candle had gone out. The second floor's lanterns must have weakened, maybe one run out of oil.

But a glow stood behind the railing. Or the echo of a glow. Some light had floated there and then vanished as Annette looked up. She must have caught the chandelier's glare in her eyes as she turned. There was no one upstairs right now to light and douse lanterns and then disappear.

The sound of scraping cloth dragged her attention to the banister, where Balthazar pressed his spine firmly against the staircase. His tracing finger drooped from one coat-planted bullet hole. No amount of prodding would heal him, but he must have known that.

"I see," he said, his head sinking. "I haven't sacrificed enough. To be blessed with God's might is to open oneself to Him. The angels will bridge the way between here and Heaven." He snatched the crucifix-dagger from the floor. "But I must consecrate this holy path."

"You're fading," Gloria said. She sounded serene, as if she'd comforted many wanted men in their final moments. "You're dying, but you want to fight."

"Of course you would think that, but I am a man of God, and He is with me, so I should want for nothing." Balthazar glanced cold eyes her way. "That does not make me a fool of God. I did not come to this nest unarmed, but bearing that with which the Lord arms me."

"Perhaps." Gloria slid one hand to her hip. "But you did bring a dagger to a gunfight."

"I bring greater might than steel fitted to the Lord's image. I bring death. I bring the Lord's unmatched power." Balthazar gritted his teeth as he raised the crucifix-dagger overhead. His chest heaved with harsh, sticky breath.

Annette smelled copper again. No one's eyes bled, meaning Saber hadn't come back.

This was Balthazar's bloody stink. A red line ran down his chin. "Surely it was for my benefit that I suffered such anguish." He coughed out a stern voice like he probably sounded in church. "In your love, you kept me from the pit of destruction; you have put all my sins behind your back."

"I don't hear the Lord's love there," Gloria said. "Any devil can quote scripture for his purposes."

"Yes, very wise," Balthazar said. Skin squeezed his tensing knuckles. "But can any devil do this?"

The Christ-dragger swung in a savage arc and tore between Balthazar's legs. A squealing scream caught in his throat and died behind clenched teeth.

Gloria retreated to Slim, one hand clutching her

pistol's grip. Sylvia and Treasure slid toward Annette. No one stepped toward the staircase to stop this.

Balthazar worked the dagger back and forth, grunting with every jerking breath. His voice filled with a gruff need for food, sex, something the world couldn't give him, and he was taking out that absence on his soft flesh.

"For the ultimate presence," he said. "Great sacrifice. I must. Be as angels."

Wet tendons snapped beneath chewing steel. The dagger worked up his pelvis, and his abdomen, blood pouring over the wooden carving of Christ. Balthazar's belly split open, and entrails pooled in a tangled nest of damp snakes. The dagger cut up his sternum and hit his collar, and Annette tucked her hand over her mouth not to scream.

The violence and the stink and a sense of smothering reminded her too much of her blackout at the ranch before Frank's death.

Balthazar yanked the crucifix-dagger out while his throat bobbed up and down. He wiped his free hand up the dark slit and squeezed the blood into a fist overhead. Red rivers trickled between his fingers and down his wrist as if he had slit himself there, too. He let the crucifix-dagger clatter to the floor again as a reverent light filled his face. How could he still speak?

"So do not fear, for I am with you!" he shouted.

Another glob of blood spattered his face, and each crimson dot hissed and steamed. Golden fire flared through his bloody coat, some oil lantern glowing in his entrails. His every twitch stoked the ragged light, and it shined brighter until the sun seemed to pour down his gory chasm and push out another twisted knot of innards. They piled onto the floor in swirling ropes.

He never glanced at the roiling tubes, like he didn't need those organs anymore, not when this golden radiance filled him in their place. Yellow light surged behind his teeth. Blood and spit burned away in plumes of white steam. The shine flared, and Treasure shielded her eyes.

"Do not be dismayed!" Smoke coiled around Balthazar's rising voice. He jerked up against the staircase on limp legs as if some unseen hand guided him to his feet. His speech grated in a broken roar. "FOR. I. AM. YOUR. GOD."

Each word clawed deep into Annette's ears, squeezing her skull tight. She wasn't meant to hear this voice—these voices? She couldn't tell. Nothing sounded right, nothing looked right, Balthazar wasn't right. He was a mountain now, his presence filling Slim's Respite to the roof and beyond.

"I. WILL. STRENGTHEN. YOU." Balthazar's golden glow hardened around him.

Gloria faltered backward as light gleamed off her revolver, and she fanned the hammer. Four pounding shots screamed through the saloon.

The blasts muffled under Balthazar's deafening chaos. Two rounds struck the wall behind him and broke black holes into the wood. The other bullets struck his twisting flesh, leaving new sagging wounds, but if they bothered him, he didn't show it.

His inner light sharpened to blinding. "AND. HELP. YOU."

Shadows flitted against this new sunrise. A hand shoved Annette toward the front entrance. She couldn't see through the glare, but she knew which way, and heard the swinging doors creak outward. Slim shouted something about running now, everyone, but his voice shrank beneath the preacher's monstrous bellowing.

"I. WILL. UPHOLD. YOU."

White afterglow filled Annette's eyes even in the outside's welcoming darkness. Bright light rushed through the swinging doors after her, and Balthazar roared too loud for anyone to call to each other.

"WITH. MY. RIGHTEOUS. HAND."

Annette couldn't see where she was going, whose hand grabbed her, or whose arm she grabbed. She could only hold tight and hope the night would hide them.

Not everyone. Ducking across the street from Slim's brought Sylvia and Treasure huddling close. No Slim. No Gloria. Where had they gone? Annette hadn't meant for them to split up. No one would want them separated except Balthazar.

"Where?" Sylvia asked.

Beyond Slim's Respite, the windows and doors of Low's Bend stood dark, the same as when Annette had ridden in on Big Pete. Only Slim had kept his lights on, and now a new ferocious luminance burst from his doorway and threw coiling shadows across the scrabbly dirt street. Unlit houses watched Sylvia drag Annette, and Annette drag Treasure. They were squat homes and businesses built of wood and dust, their slanted awnings guarding low porches against daily sunshine. They kept their doorways hidden from moonlight and starlight alike. None were ready for Balthazar.

Annette couldn't remember who lived in the building directly across the street, but next door to it stood Arch's house. Treasure led that way. He had to be hiding in the dark, and he could hide them, too.

"He's a witch," Treasure hissed.

"A witch preacher?" Annette asked.

"A witch for Christ." Treasure had a cry in her voice. "Oh, Jesus."

Sylvia turned back and shushed them. She had almost reached the far side of the street when a rush of cold wind sent her cringing and stumbling. Annette tripped and lost her grip on Treasure, who hit the dirt on hands and knees, her petticoat shredding on one side.

"Jesus," she whimpered. "Jesus, please."

Annette turned back to grab her again, but the light froze her in place.

Balthazar strode from the porch of Slim's Respite. A luminous pillar stretched up his center from groin to throat, whiting out every detail within his black silhouette.

"Jesus Christ is in Heaven!" he bellowed. "But I stand in His place in this world until His righteous rebirth."

CRUEL ANGELS PAST SUNDOWN

His voice rattled the glass in window frames, and a tremor quaked in Annette's jaw. This outburst should have brought townsfolk rushing to their porches, curious about the angry shouting and sudden sunshine in the middle of the night. White smoke poured from Balthazar's clothes, eyes, mouth, as if he'd eaten glowing dust. A curling plume streamed toward around the brim of his hat and beyond the roof of Slim's Respite, toward cloud-blotted moon and stars.

And something else.

The few visible constellations rippled as if Annette were staring at the sky's reflection in a puddle rather than the sky itself. Stillness dripped from the heavens across her, an inescapable sense of being watched.

Another circle had replaced the moon, some great crooked eye in the night, pearlescent and transparent. Faint patterns fluttered in a halo around it, almost words, as if a scrivener had spread the sky across a writing desk and scribbled notes in starlit ink.

"An eye," Annette whispered.

Sylvia tugged Annette's arm, tearing her attention down. When she glanced skyward again, the night hid whatever she'd seen.

There was only Balthazar.

Another tug and Annette staggered from the street. She thrashed one hand around Treasure's forearm and pulled up. They had to make it inside Arch's, maybe out his back door, hide in some other house. Balthazar had to know where they were headed now, but getting out of sight mattered most.

Treasure wouldn't move. She hunkered to the ground on all fours, and every part of her trembled.

Sylvia pulled; Annette did the same. Her fingers slipped from Treasure's glove, grasped at empty air, and then she was stumbling backward toward Arch's porch. Sylvia wouldn't stand here and die, wouldn't stop pulling. Annette thought to tear her arm away, grab Treasure by the waist, and haul her toward Arch's front door.

But Balthazar had crossed the street already. To stop would mean letting him catch up. Annette quit fighting against Sylvia, and their two-woman caravan broke for Arch's porch.

Balthazar's smoking boots stopped beside Treasure. "I made the mistake of mercy before," he said. "This, I will not repeat. Damned is damned. If you will live in the absence of God, you will dwell bereft of Him forever. Hell awaits."

Treasure swiveled toward him. Her face was a mask of tears.

Balthazar reached for her chin and tilted her gaze upward. "Tell me your name, child of God."

Porch planks shifted beneath Annette's feet. She couldn't tear her gaze from Balthazar's white glow, how it reflected in Treasure's wet cheeks, her glittering eyes. If only she would stand.

But she whimpered instead. "Treasure."

"No false names before the might of the Lord," Balthazar said. "Shed sin from your tongue and reveal to me your Christian name."

"Clara." Treasure coughed out a sob. "Buckhurst."

Balthazar's weathered hand stroked the tears from her cheeks. "Be not afraid, Clara Buckhurst, for your life of sin now ends."

Hinges creaked, and Annette thought of Saber—no, it was Sylvia thrusting open Arch's front door. Annette slipped back and felt the house take her, meaning to shield her from this nightmare. All she had to do was turn around, and face its darkness with the echo of Balthazar's light branded on her eyes.

Balthazar stroked Treasure's jawline. "Love you the Lord?" he asked.

Treasure's bottom lip quivered. "Yes." She was frail beneath Balthazar's smoke.

He slid his hand toward her temple. "Speak your love."

"I love the Lord," Treasure said. Her voice was wet and thick, and her eyelids squeezed tight.

CRUEL ANGELS PAST SUNDOWN

"Then rejoice, creature of the night, for your love is rewarded," Balthazar said. His palm flattened over the top of her head. "And in this moment, you enter the kingdom of God."

His chest's radiance dimmed, but it was not dead. A snake of light coiled through his shoulder, down his arm, and into his hand, where it poured white-hot tongues through Treasure's scalp. Her eyes tore wide open, and smoke poured from inside them. A ragged scream swelled in her throat and chased a smoldering plume through her teeth, meeting and mixing with Balthazar's dusty aura. If he'd kept a thousand fireflies in the back of his mouth minutes earlier, then ten times as many shined past Treasure's lips, as if she'd swallowed a smith's forge.

Her skin sloughed in the white light. Bones crunched beneath Balthazar's fingers. Treasure's head shriveled beneath the shine of a molten sunrise searing down her shoulders and corset, and her scream melted into a fading hiss.

Annette wrenched her head into the dark house, and the door swung too late to hide Treasure as her body crumbled in a heap of smoking ash.

TEN:
DARK HOUSES

A RCH'S FRONT DOOR sealed out the worst of Balthazar's light, but a hazy glow still outlined the frame and flickered through the windows. Not enough to properly reveal the insides of the house, but shadows flashed from every wooden column, stairway post, and furniture leg through the narrow parlor, as if fragments of people surrounded Annette.

There was only Sylvia. Her eye formed a white circle in the dark and reminded Annette too much of the visage she'd seen above Low's Bend moments ago. She must have imagined it. Being caught up in Balthazar's impossibility had made her dream of other impossible sights.

But then, she'd dismissed that lantern glow in his throat and eyes earlier, only for the light to turn monstrous through the rest of him.

"Did he see us sneak away?" Sylvia asked.

Annette shook her head, not a *no*, but an *I don't know*. Would Sylvia tell the difference? Annette didn't know that, either.

The outside glow washed across Sylvia's eyepatch. "What's he want?"

"What he sees," Annette said.

Balthazar was unfocused. He had followed Saber to the ranch, believing her womb ripe with God, but he'd turned his attention to Annette, too. Slim, Gloria, Treasure—they had each taken his eyes at some moment. And he'd taken Treasure's eyes, her skin, her life. She was right. He was a witch. The kind who praised Christ and served death, while she had never hurt a soul, dealing out no worse harm than a broken heart. Patient, kind, and a fellow keeper of secrets.

Now she was dust, not even a body to bury.

"I should've held her wrist tighter," Annette said. Her hand was a white claw in the dark.

"I should have stopped," Sylvia said. She sounded aghast with disbelief. "She didn't deserve this."

Annette's dim view rippled. "No, she didn't." She had no tears, only a hissing rage inside, but she had to keep this fire locked behind its furnace door. If she let it drive her screaming again at Balthazar, she would only be handing herself over to him.

"You don't find friends like her just anywhere." Sylvia leaned close in the dark. "Didn't he know that? Couldn't he tell? There won't ever be someone like her. I should've told him. That would've stopped him."

Annette wrapped both arms around Sylvia's shoulders and held her close. "He wouldn't listen. Likes to hear himself talk too much. Ain't nothing you could have done."

They held together a moment, and then Annette broke away, pressed Sylvia's hand, and took cautious steps deeper into the parlor. She didn't know Arch well, had never stepped inside his house before. Meager light traced the edges of wall shelves, the fireplace, and an armoire.

"Arch?" Annette whispered. No answer.

Except for Balthazar. The walls muffled his bellowing, but the message was clear—he was on the hunt. Annette had been too stubborn for his dagger to kill her, yet she was never fierce enough to stop him with a lashing shotgun or a stream of curses. Even Gloria's bullets had curled around him, or been swallowed by his skin, little worse than horseflies.

If he found Annette, he would cook her skull from the

inside out until she fell to ashes, and then he'd carry on following Saber, expectant for a coming birth.

The child would not be a new Christ on Earth. Whatever grew beneath that skin had made her sick inside. Annette couldn't guess what, didn't want to know. She wanted to be a thousand miles from Low's Bend.

"Arch," Sylvia whispered. Not a question or a call.

Annette peered at a dining table not far into the next room, its surface littered with metal pieces. Arch had been taking apart his rifles, no clear reason why.

Beneath the table lay Arch himself.

No firearm laid in his hands, and it wouldn't have saved him from Saber anyway. Her drowsy aura clouded all sense of self-preservation. He lay on his back, arms at his sides, grim blotches patterning his clothing around a gaping canyon up his center.

The red nightmare dripped down Annette's thoughts. Its substance pooled in jagged torso wounds, cracked sternums, and cut-out organs.

Sylvia raised a hand over her mouth and nose. "We can't stay."

She was right. The light brightened around dark corners. Between this radiance and the creaking steps outside, Balthazar had to be searching. Saber, too.

Annette patted along scarcely visible walls, leading Sylvia this time until they reached the back door. It opened on a small patch of brush bordered by stunted wooden fencing. The house cast a deep shadow behind it, its front bathed in Balthazar's light.

What about Gloria? Slim? Balthazar might've already given them the same death he'd given to Treasure. How long did he take to burn each skull and body to dust?

Annette couldn't think like that. If she believed the others were dead, she would fall right here. Best to traipse thoughtlessly through weeds and thorns, over the short fence, toward the Calhoun house next door. A narrow house, its fencing set it back from the street, and Annette led Sylvia around to the porch and toward the front door. They didn't glance Balthazar's way in case he might catch their eyes in the dark. The door stood unlocked, and they slipped inside.

This house was darker than the last and held a sour odor. Annette wished for a lantern or candle, but the light would draw Balthazar. Better he stumble lost through Low's Bend. Let him wander the whole world before he had any reason to check the Calhoun house.

"Mr. Calhoun?" Annette whispered. She wished she could remember his first name. Had she ever known it? She wasn't sure she'd known anything before tonight.

A muffled scream dragged Annette into the dim sitting room. Sylvia stood before a fireplace, both hands at her face this time. How she had found anything in the dark was a mystery, but now that she'd pointed out her discovery, Annette saw them—two bodies draping the dusty floorboards.

There was a man in long pajamas, his chest torn open, and a woman with her nightgown cut the same. Dark stains soaked their clothing, and chasms opened their sternums and bellies, sources of the house's odor.

Annette sank beside them. "Mrs. Calhoun?"

"She's gone," Sylvia said, hands still partway covering her mouth. "They're gone."

Annette grasped Mrs. Calhoun's hand, but the fingers were stiff, stuck curled into a claw. She had fallen under Saber's spell and received no mercy.

"We'll try the next house," Annette said.

Sylvia stepped back. "The Barkers."

"She couldn't have got everyone in town." Annette dropped Mrs. Calhoun's hand. "We'll try."

"The Barkers have children," Sylvia whispered. A strangled whine slid up her throat. "I can't see little ones. Like that. Like this!"

"It can't be everyone," Annette said, sterner now.

But then, Low's Bend was not a large town. Slow as Saber might walk, she had wandered back and forth from

Slim's Respite twice. Worse, who could say she had gone there first? Annette might have lay blacked out for hours while Saber carved her way through the sleeping town, and everyone in Slim's Respite might have been oblivious until Annette woke up and told her story. The red nightmare had swallowed her time, her thoughts.

It swallowed her now, as if she were face-first plunging into these carved ravines of still-warm gore. The world was gristle, bone, and meat. There was no hope. If Saber hadn't already cut these people open, Balthazar would have come burning. The dead had it easy. No more tension, terror, love, any of it.

Low's Bend was not a large town, sure, but its street and houses could fit a lifetime of misery in a single night. What a special place.

And deep within the red, Annette made out a face. She'd seen Saber's pallid cheeks and empty eyes in the nightmare before, but here came someone new to the vision, yet plenty familiar. Deep creases worked down his face, and a smile curled his mustache as if he were readying to make Annette laugh.

But there was no laughter in the red nightmare. Not when Frank crawled through his own insides, through Annette's mind, and reached for her.

"Annie!" Sylvia snapped.

Annette's eyelids dragged against heavy sinew. She hadn't realized she'd shut them, and now they didn't want to open. The night hung red and dark.

She sat bent over her knees, face hovering inches from Mrs. Calhoun's stained dress and the thick hot stink of her insides. Both hands had plunged into the torn fabric and this warm cavern as if fishing for the same meat Saber had hungered for in Frank. Something fat and wet filled Annette's mouth, and she found a third limb stretching down her chest toward the flesh her hands had dug up, its end fingerless and curling.

No, not a limb—her overgrown tongue.

ELEVEN:
INFECTION

ANNETTE GASPED HER tongue back behind her teeth. It shrank against the bottom of her mouth as if it was always a flat little worm and never a curving red snake.

She wrenched her arms from the body's warm muck and fell back onto her hands and knees. Her fingertips squeaked against the worn floorboards, leaving bloody handprints. A flicker passed over one window and shined briefly across her forearm, where dark blood stained partway down her wrist. The rest of her arm glowed pale at the light's edge. Not quite Saber's pallor, but somewhere between Annette's usual sun-kissed tone and that bone-white flesh.

"Pale mark," Sylvia said. She retreated deeper into the house, her shape flitting through shadows. "Like the madman said. What he did to his daughter, she's passed it onto you."

Annette flexed her stained hand. Beneath the blood, what color were her fingers? Gone pale as Treasure's skin? As her ashes—as Saber? Annette imagined herself staggering across the prairie with a creaking wooden house in her throat, some spectral legend that gunslingers and travelers might pass around the campfire, only without a cavalry saber at her side or a baby in her belly. No one would confuse her for Saber.

Annette never liked ghost stories. They always ended with a wandering spirit in lingering death. Unfinished tales.

She pressed her hands to the floorboards and staggered to her feet. "Sylvia?" Heavy wood clunked at the back of the house, and she followed the noise.

Sylvia pawed frantically around unseen furniture. The darkness had to be hard on her remaining eye, and dried hunks of tree and pieces of half-finished chairs scattered the way to the back door. She knocked them left and right to reach it and then screamed as she reached another body lying slumped on the floor. She skirted around it.

Annette couldn't tell who it used to be and didn't have time to care. "Sylvia, wait."

"Don't follow," Sylvia said. Her shrill voice scratched toward panic. "You stay here."

"With the dead?" Annette asked. "It ain't a curse. Just sickness, like pox."

"And I won't have it." Sylvia knocked another crude chair aside and reached the wall. Palms slapped wood as she searched for the door.

"She did something to me. It won't catch like that." Annette reached into the darkness. "Sylvia, it's me."

"It's nothing natural," Sylvia said. "You're marked. He said so, you heard him." She fumbled at the doorknob, and the hinges squealed. "Damned is damned."

Something in her accusation made Annette bristle, and she charged into the dark. "And all the secrets we keep?" she snapped. "That means nothing? That it? Because you're afraid of me now?"

"It means something." Sylvia's figure formed in silhouette as she swung open the back door, carving a tall brick of light into the wall. "And this means something else. I never betrayed you, but you need to keep away from me. Right now."

Stars shined in scant dots, their sky almost entirely blotted with clouds, but Balthazar's light cast the Calhoun house's shadow across the back of its property. Sylvia stumbled down two steps and into the soil, where broken chairs littered the earth as if Mr. Calhoun had been trying to plant and grow them. Jutting legs snagged her petticoat, but they couldn't stop her.

Annette braced the doorway. If she called out, Balthazar might hear. She couldn't blame Sylvia for her panic. If Annette hadn't already watched Frank die under Saber's blade, watching Treasure burn might have destroyed all sense of togetherness for her, too.

"But it's still me," Annette whispered, looking down. "Ain't it?"

There was enough light when she glanced over herself to make out the discolored streaks where Balthazar's dagger had bloodied her dress. The wound felt strange beneath, itchy like it had already scarred over. It hadn't killed her, so it saw no point in persisting.

Balthazar would do worse if he caught her again. If anything unnatural walked tonight, it was him. And his daughter. Not Annette. None of this was her fault. Those two strangers had stumbled onto her family ranch and dragged all their problems with them. Sylvia couldn't blame them on Annette, even if she'd in turn dragged them to Low's Bend.

But if Balthazar was right about a sickness between her and Saber, what else was he right about? Angels speaking to him? An immaculate conception? Some holy crusade?

Annette couldn't accept it. "Sylvia!" she hissed. She lifted her dress and hurried down the steps.

Sylvia slowed midway through the garden of two-foot dowels and misshapen chair legs.

"I won't hurt you." Annette reached the soil. A chair leg snagged her dress's hem and tore through the stiff fabric. "Please, don't leave me."

Sylvia didn't glance back, and Annette realized she hadn't stopped over any desperate plea.

A figure interrupted the dirt. Darkness had almost

consumed all her traces, but Balthazar's light shimmered off her bloodied skin.

Sylvia twisted on one leg, swallowed a squeaking cry, and then limped to the right. Likely toward a neighboring house. Her cheek gleamed in the light, wetted by bloody tears. Her footsteps faded beneath a distant rumbling tempest as if the night sky were taking a deep breath.

Annette's legs wouldn't turn and follow. The figure in the dirt kept her set in place.

Both figures. One lay in a pile of shattered wood, where Mr. Calhoun must have snapped at one misbehaving almost-chair and taken a hatchet to the wood, chopping until it lay in splinters at his property's edge. Had that hatchet stood anywhere in sight, Annette would have grabbed it, but she couldn't have said what she would do next.

The body was Mortimer. He didn't belong here. He lived somewhere farther from the saloon as if he'd made a habit of walking off his night drinking.

But he'd died here, and there would be no more drink for him. A cavalry saber had cut open his guts and chest, wrenched up his sternum, and cut loose precious pieces inside. They draped the soil, fresh additions to the garden of broken chairs, to perhaps grow a new Mortimer. His face gawked up at the blackening sky, faint light catching in the whites of his eyes. No one had shut them.

No one had shut Frank's, either, if Saber hadn't.

Annette could ask now. She didn't expect a *yes* or *no*. The question would hang in the air, answered only by a throaty groan. But she could try asking.

Saber gazed across the garden, her face painted with gore.

TWELVE:
PREGNANT WITH SIN

THE RED NIGHTMARE might as well take over. Its smothering weight would make the night easier to bear. Let it win, let Annette dance to this sickness while her mind sank into a damp crimson hell. Frank was there, inside himself, in her. Waiting.

The dark sky swelled, almost becoming that red curtain, but Annette surfaced from the nightmare to watch a white stalk grow across the splinter-laden soil.

Saber was rising. Her snakish tongue tore across the back of her free hand, lapping at a dark stain. She must have cleaned herself this catlike way after bathing in Frank's insides, too. Her blade hung to one side as she staggered over Mortimer's body, and it clacked against jutting chair legs at every other step.

Strange warmth curled in Annette's skin. She should run. Saber might not go easy this time, might carve Annette's chest open and dig out her organs, defile her corpse. That was Saber's way.

But she had already infected Annette. The mark of a sickly pallor, the worming tongue, the nightmare where Frank squatted toadlike in a pond of blood.

"What'd you do to me?" Annette asked.

Her voice scarcely whispered out, little louder than a hiss, and she couldn't be sure she'd said anything at all. Was it like that for Saber? Maybe every dry groan meant she was trying to speak, and no one could understand. Maybe someone rested in her head. Not Frank, but a dead lover or Wilcox relative. Someone special to Saber.

Her blade struck another chair leg as she reached Annette. The wooden creaking climbed her throat in a two-tone note.

"Lkmm."

Were those almost words? Mischief sometimes lived in the wind and played tricks on the ears. Annette remembered a door hinge at the ranch that used to cry like a cow in labor, and there was a settling floorboard at Slim's Respite that seemed to ask, *Whaaat?* Meaningless noises pretending at speech.

But the groan came again, inches from Annette's face, and unmistakable words crackled between Saber's lips.

"Like. Me."

Like her. In what way? That they were alike, or that Saber wanted Annette's approval? Annette opened her mouth to ask.

And Saber jammed their lips together.

Annette stiffened and yanked her head back, but a too-long tongue shot between her teeth and filled her mouth, an invasive snake seeking a hole in the ground where she might lay her eggs.

As if Saber thought she could regurgitate her unborn child up her throat, down Annette's, and into a new womb.

The world went red. Saber had seen this nightmare first and shared it, but it was a lonely place, one nobody else in the world could feel. Annette had stopped fighting. The tongue's soft tip caressed while its root fattened between Annette's teeth. Saber would fill her throat and body with sweated copper. The nightmare bubbled, recognizing its source.

A rot lived in Saber, ancient like Annette couldn't imagine. Her own red nightmare might decay if she let this infectious kiss go on, a new sin impregnating her. Frank would know inside her and take it as a greater reason for haunting her head. One more guilt added to pretending remorse for their lack of children, for abandoning him to die. His soul wouldn't move on to any paradise or pit, but squat inside her, exactly as she deserved.

Her furnace door screeched open at the back of her throat and poured fire into her skull. She wrenched hard and broke away as a sick wet shriek tore up Saber's throat.

"Stop that!" Annette snapped.

Saber retreated a clumsy step, bent over her swollen belly, and vomited a dark sludge. It spilled between broken chair legs and formed a sinewy black puddle. Her eating of people's flesh and licking up their blood might have been a strange craving, some odd mix of carrying a child and wearing the mark Balthazar had cast on her, but she was still human under there, as prone to illness as anyone.

Her eyes wandered over the lumps in the soil, and then over Annette as if she could do something about the mess. About anything.

Saber groaned, stretching out another two words. "Let. Me."

"Let you what?" Annette asked, her throat tensing. "I don't know what you want, but it ain't me. Hurting me more won't help you."

"Hurt," Saber said, another drawn-out croak as one hand stroked her round middle. "Me. Hurt me."

Annette watched the pale skin where those fingers traced. *Getting put up with a child we didn't want?* Slim had said. *It could happen to any of us.*

Annette tightened her fists at her sides, and fire lashed beneath her inner furnace door. She'd felt the same furious surge when she railed against Balthazar in the saloon. This family seemed to draw up the worst in her, father and daughter alike. The baby would be no different.

"Wanted me to hurt you, so you killed Frank, that it?" Annette asked. "Why didn't you hurt yourself instead and leave us alone?"

Saber stroked her gut again and shook her head. "See.

Red." Her head lolled dreamily to one side. Her blade cut a line in the dirt.

Annette had watched this exhaustion weigh on her husband's limbs in the ranch house, and on Mortimer in the saloon. She had felt it tug her down, first to drowsy darkness and then the red nightmare. The same would take Saber's thoughts and drown them face down in her mind's river.

Whether or not Balthazar was the source of the pregnancy, he was certainly the source of this suffocating nightmare and this murderous curse. If Saber tried to hurt herself, or the baby, her thoughts would drown. Every other horror spread from there.

The fire fumed up Annette's throat and onto her lengthening tongue. "And you had to spread this to me?"

She licked dry lips, coppery with Saber's strange kiss. That couldn't have been the first they'd shared. Darkness had come to her in the ranch house, the fat swelling of a tongue. A pale mark had passed between two women. Saber must have meant to tear it off her skin and throw it onto Annette, but she'd only dirtied them both. There was no shortage of soil in this world. Sickness wouldn't migrate, only reproduce.

Saber stepped past the pile of innards. "Hurt. Me."

"I get it was wrong, whatever happened to you, but that didn't mean you had to hurt me with it," Annette said. Her teeth clenched so tight they might crack. "Didn't have to hurt all these people. My husband. My Frank!"

"Hurt. Me."

Saber had seemed more a wild animal than a woman at the ranch. Annette could be wilder. Angrier. Bloodier.

"You cut him open!" she snapped. "He didn't deserve it. Understand? He was a good man, and you don't got a clue what that even is, what he meant to me!"

Saber croaked again. "Hurt. Me."

Annette's limbs trembled with heat, and her mouth was a boiling swamp. Thrashing against Balthazar in the saloon, she hadn't recognized the fire as hers, but this fury no longer felt like a foreign seed planted inside her. There had always been rage, as if she were born with it, and there had always been a furnace door she had learned to keep shut.

The door was young, and the fury was old, burned into her blood since before memory. The pale mark knew it as kin.

"Hurt you, hurt you," Annette chanted. "Fine! You can't hurt yourself, then I'll do it."

Saber groaned. "Do. It."

One hand flexed into a claw, the other wrenched a broken chair leg from the earth, and Annette launched screaming at Saber.

The chair leg slid from her hand, and her claw swiped at empty air. Both knees jellied. The world teetered beneath her, rocking like a ship on strange tides. That howling storm beyond Low's Bend had to be drawing off some sudden coast, torn unnaturally across the prairie to wash Annette into the red nightmare.

Frank stared from beneath a thick sinewy curtain. He did not look like himself, his chest a cavern of horrors. He needed a loving touch, a kiss on his mustache, a repentant wife who would beg his forgiveness. He had always bent to her needs. What had she done when he needed her but stare blankly while steel cut through his stomach, heart, and lungs?

"Do. It."

Smothering oceans sloughed from Annette's head. The creaking came again, and Saber sounded more like a door hinge now than ever, two painful notes first rising and then falling. Rising. *Do*. Falling. *It*.

Saber cocked her head to one side as her sword caught distant light. "Do. It."

Annette scrabbled through the dirt toward the Calhoun house. Her legs kept buckling at each backward kick. Why did the nightmare sometimes smother, and other times pulsate? The fire inside set it thrashing, but Saber wanted to make everyone docile. To help her, do as she liked, but they couldn't hurt her no matter what she wanted. She had known the nightmare longest; had been sick with it for weeks or months. Had she spread it to anyone else, Balthazar must have already killed them.

But not Annette.

She staggered to her feet and hobbled toward the yard's end, her dress tearing on shattered wooden chunks. A path opened between houses, back toward the street. The farther she walked from Saber, the better she could think.

"Do. It." Saber's blade clanged against the Calhoun house's wall. "Do. It."

Annette darted around the next corner, onto the porch, to the far side facing Arch's home, where she slid into the soil between houses.

The wind chased. Footsteps. A moaning throat caked in dried blood. "Do. It."

Annette glanced at her hands. One flexed into a claw, fingers gloved in gore. The fury cooked the red nightmare into a frothing pit. It demanded Annette give herself.

Saber craved the pain, but the mark forbid it. She handed out suffering and death as if inflicting these miseries might earn her way to firsthand experience. She was little more than a mindless wanderer, with no thought, knowledge, or future, only intent.

And some grief. There was maybe shame, too.

Annette knew the feeling. Frank had come crawling through the nightmare, and now he sat in a pool in her head, but he might creep closer, might catch her. *Didn't I give you everything?* he would ask, his mustache crusted with blood. *But you couldn't give me the truth.*

A hollering climbed several houses down—Balthazar shouting about sin and the Lord. Annette couldn't make out the exact words.

"Do," Saber croaked, but she didn't finish her couplet. One foot ground against soil and then scraped away. The next steps faded deeper into Low's Bend. Headed for Balthazar.

Annette placed a hand over her heart. Her wound had calmed. She slid her fingers beneath her dress and stroked tender skin, scarred shut as if Balthazar had stabbed her days ago. Another symptom of this strange infection, or had the night been so endless?

It wouldn't end if she sat here. The sickness would turn her into a wandering naked murderer.

She pressed her back to the outer wall and strained her legs to stand again. The night hung dark now, Balthazar's light hidden by other houses while the stars had vanished behind rolling clouds. A beast lurked in the northern wind and roared across the prairie.

Something soft rustled across the street, mixing soil with Treasure's ashes, and Annette turned to Slim's Respite as two tumbleweeds rolled past the frail light ebbing through the doorway and windows.

All the noise had hidden arguing whispers. Not inside the saloon or up in the boarding rooms, but near. Annette sagged backward, almost falling, and then thrust ahead toward the voices.

She knew them.

THIRTEEN:
HEAVENLY NEED

THE SHED STOOD behind Slim's Respite, a flimsy low-roofed bundle of wood kept aloft by a few nails and some counterweight of roof and wall that Annette didn't understand. Dust caked the surface, patterned by handprints.

Slim crouched ahead of a shut narrow door, where he fiddled with a padlock. The bending made his breath hard, and blood oozed through Treasure's scarf, bound around his thigh. Gloria crouched beside him, her hat pressed low.

Alive. Not skulls burned out, not ashes, but alive.

Annette charged toward the shed. The wind rumbled north of town, hints of Mortimer's predicted dust storm, but Slim's and Gloria's voices came clear without the saloon blocking them off. They must have kept quiet until Balthazar passed.

"—can't cut out his tongue," Slim said. "Can't touch him, can't shut him up."

"You watched me shoot him," Gloria said. "You watched. Four bullets, not a scratch."

"Four is nothing." Slim clutched a key in one hand, but its jiggling and scraping didn't seem to please the unhappy padlock. "What I got in here will be bigger, better, if this bastard would turn."

"I hunt men, Slim. He's something worse." Gloria shook her head. "Much worse." Her eyes glittered in looking past Slim's shoulder, toward Annette, and she stiffened to her feet. "Who goes?"

Annette glanced down at herself. Couldn't Gloria see? The skin had paled, and the arms wore dark residue from fingers to wrists, but this dress was the same, with its dried stains down one side. Annette's hair, her face—didn't any features matter? It was the night hiding her. In daylight, Gloria would see.

Would Slim and Gloria act the same as Sylvia, casting Annette out as a marked demon? Balthazar was powerful, but she refused to believe he could ravage their souls the same as their bodies. More than that, Annette had to believe she could crawl out of Saber's sickness and find herself again.

And believe this night would end.

"It's me," Annette said, taking another step. If Gloria had drawn her gun, it didn't show in the dark. "Annette."

"Butterfly." Gloria swept her arms around Annette's shoulders in a hard embrace and stroked her back and hair. "Knew I didn't lose you."

Annette stopped herself from reaching back, her hovering, her trembling hands like two confused flies left buzzing with nowhere to land. Red-brown splotches coated her fingers and congealed beneath her fingernails. While blood had splattered Gloria's clothes in her line of work, none of it had been Annette's fault, and she didn't want to change that now.

She shrank from Gloria's arms. "Why haven't you two run?"

"Our big bright man would notice the two of us mounting up," Gloria said, tilting her head at Slim's Respite. The stables stood slanted-roofed beside the saloon, where Big Pete sheltered alongside a few townsfolk horses and Gloria's white gelding. "Besides, I wouldn't leave you. And Slim here allegedly has a plan. He keeps some secret inside, ought to turn the night around for us."

"Not mine," Slim said. He yanked the key from the

padlock, blew twice into the keyhole, and jammed in the key again. "Keepsake belonged to Arch. But it might be mine now."

A man's chest cracked open behind Annette's eyes. "Arch?" she asked.

"I'm doubtful myself," Gloria said. "I asked, 'What the blazes is Arch supposed to do, drink the bastard to death?' And Slim tells me—"

"You'll see." Slim crooked the key up and down.

Annette had watched a blade do the same, stuck in Frank's chest. The red nightmare flashed through her head, a wasteland of blood around Frank's face, and she bit her lip to keep down a scream and worse. She wouldn't tell Slim or Gloria that Arch was dead. If they weren't going to flee Low's Bend and leave Balthazar to his dust and sermons, they needed to focus. Even more so if they had a chance at stopping him.

"We want what Arch keeps back here," Slim said, grunting. His wrist gave a sharp turn, and the reluctant padlock coughed an iron cry. He tore the key from the lock, flung the latch, and shoved the door open. "A little old, but it might work."

Gloria left Annette and looked over Slim's shoulder. "Worth a try, I say."

The already-meager light scarcely reached inside the shed. If a lantern hung inside the door, Annette didn't see it. Likely Slim never planned to visit the shed at night.

A harsh cloud puffed from the doorway as he pushed inside. He hadn't been cleaning the cramped space, only opening it whenever he had some new piece of junk to toss inside and lock away. The darkness suggested shelves, shovels, glass bottles, and the rim of a steel drum, where he might have been brewing his own liquor, or at least storing it.

A larger mystery hunkered to one side, where a dust-coated linen sheet covered a shaft half the length of Annette's body. One wooden wheel stuck out partway from underneath; another shaped the sheet in a tented lump.

"Is it a cannon?" Annette asked.

"Better," Slim said.

He unfolded the sheet from the partly covered wheel, and his plan took form in the night. A wild idea after watching Balthazar's body swallow whole bullets, something Annette had never thought she would see.

But then, she had never seen this contraption before either. Her closest experience with firearms came from handling Frank's rifle for scaring off coyotes. Sometimes she imagined Gloria's gunfights with two or three murderers at a time.

No haphazard shots at the ranch or showdowns on the roads beyond Low's Bend seemed fit for this grim creation, and yet Arch had hidden it here anyway.

Maybe he and all men were mistaken when they brought it to wars and massacres. This contraption was never meant for people. Its creator must have known a night of monsters would come.

Somewhere in town, one monster roared. "I only need her—Annette Ruthie Klein!"

Slim kept his eyes on the weapon's shaft, one hand teasing at the circle of cylinders and then patting the slot where the gun would swallow shells and spit out their casings.

"My daughter has spread the mark to no one else in your little town," Balthazar went on. "Leave this one woman, and you will live."

Gloria glanced back, lips pursed. There were sometimes miles between people, even when they stood five feet apart. Annette couldn't blame anyone for walking away and leaving her to this mad preacher, not when she'd led him and his daughter to Low's Bend in the first place.

A loving hand reached across those miles anyway as Gloria squeezed Annette's shoulder. "It'll be alright, Butterfly." She turned to Slim and asked, "What do we do to get this bloody beast firing?"

Slim shoved the lid from a wooden crate and peered

inside. "Haul it out, run up the rounds." He spread sweat-painted cheeks in an oversized grin. "Pray it won't explode in our faces."

Pray. To God? He had supposedly charged Balthazar on this crusade of blood and death, so what good was praying?

Annette turned from the shed to the dark shape of Slim's Respite, where Treasure's upstairs window glowed as if someone were alive up there. The remaining candle seemed wrong when another light had killed her. She deserved the peace of darkness.

White-gold smoke plumed from down the street as if Balthazar were carting around a campfire of molten dust. Annette watched it twist skyward, where it might meet black clouds. If it joined them, she didn't see.

The writing stole her gaze. Golden script slid through the sky in graceful curls. At their center, the white orb had returned, glistening as wet as Sylvia's eye in the gloominess of Low's Bend houses, but with none of her terror or humanity. This suggestion of an eye hovered unloving and watchful, its gaze sticking to Annette, to everyone. Especially Balthazar.

"Understand this!" he bellowed, jerking Annette's eyes from the sky. "We were chosen. The angels opened Heaven to bring their gift to my daughter. A new Annunciation."

A hard wind cut between behind Slim's Respite and through Annette's tattered dress. She pressed her arms to her sides; she wouldn't hug herself with these soiled hands. Her eyes flickered up again, but the white orb—a giant eye or something else—had vanished, an eyelid of night closing with heavy anticipation. The golden script faded from its circle.

Annette blinked hard as if that would bring the vision back. What was she seeing up there? What the hell could it mean? Tonight had been too strange between Saber and Balthazar for that apparition in the sky to be a coincidence.

Something had come to Low's Bend to watch the night unfold. Did Balthazar know?

His voice again rang out. "And they said unto her, fear

not, for you carry the Lord. And they said unto me, be not afraid, servant of God. And they said unto the world, rejoice, for the Almighty has come." He sounded harsher now, excited, like he had found someone alive to shout at and wanted them to know it. "She is heir to Mary, mother of God. The Lord will find rebirth in His creation!"

A shrill scream shot across Low's Bend. Any other night, the townsfolk would have hopped up from their houses with curious eyes and readied firearms, but Saber had cut out too many torsos. Everyone might be dead, except for the soul behind this familiar scream, echoing again down the street.

Sylvia.

"He's found her," Annette said. "He'll hurt her like he hurt Treasure."

"Working on it." Slim had squatted on his haunches and was jimmying an iron panel against his secret weapon's underside.

"It's rather unintuitive," Gloria said. She shot a forlorn glance toward the rest of town, a scarcely visible couple rows of black shapes. "We'll have it ready soon, but if we head out there now, he'll—" Another shriek cut Gloria off. Her hand slid toward her pistol. "We'll call him this way."

Annette glanced at the trail of bright smoke. Sylvia couldn't wait. The moment Balthazar put Treasure to her knees, she had belonged to him. Saber had belonged to him, too. Far too many people had already suffered and died tonight. Annette stepped from the shed's doorway and turned.

Gloria caught her arm. Her eyes made wide white circles against her face. "No, Butterfly."

Annette glanced down at her arm. Gloria's fingers curled around pale skin. Hers were insistent fingers, full of love. Annette grasped Gloria's hand, drew it up, and kissed her palm. It was dry and dusty and sweet. She gave a reassuring squeeze.

And then she let go of Gloria and tore off toward Balthazar's smoke.

FOURTEEN:
HEIR TO THE MOTHER

FROM SLIM'S RESPITE, Annette passed the spot where poor Treasure had turned to dust—no lingering, no mourning, there wasn't time—and crossed the porch of the neighboring Smith house. The smell of its hidden bloodbath wafted through the open front door. Farther on, the cobbler's home and workshop sat quiet; Annette couldn't remember his surname, but his wife was Eliza. Next stood the empty house where the late sheriff had lived and died a sick old man.

Beyond that, Sylvia tripped and fell in the street. Balthazar's smoldering tower of light stepped a few paces behind her. Smoke belched from his ripped-up torso and coiled skyward, where the watcher's great eye hid behind stormy darkness. Annette doubted she could make it out if the eyelid were to lift. She stood too close to Balthazar now, and his radiance lit the world.

He pointed one narrow finger to fallen Sylvia. "Creature of the night." His voice was heat and fire. Maybe he had a furnace door inside him, too, everyone might, desperate to smother an innate fury they could never control. His was certainly open now.

Sylvia crawled, tried to stand, and collapsed again. She was sobbing, most of her face a damp sheen beneath the light.

Balthazar's voice stood to attention. "Tell me your name, child of God."

Sylvia squeezed her eye shut. "Sylvia Washington."

"I would see you follow your sister sinner, Sylvia Washington." The rest of Balthazar's fingers spread from his outstretched hand. "Hell awaits."

If Annette came waving her arms and shouting his name, he might suspect a trap. She kicked at the street and sucked in air with an overdone gasp as if she had stumbled upon him and Sylvia by accident and been surprised. As if people couldn't hear his self-righteous preaching across the Rocky Mountains in California.

He set down one boot and turned sharply from Sylvia. Smoke curled up his eyes and around his furrowed brow.

Annette had his attention. She was supposed to run again. Past the derelict house, the cobbler's, the Smith house, to Slim's Respite and the shed behind.

Her feet wouldn't obey. Muscles twinged through her thighs and down her legs, where her heel scuffed the street. She could have worn through the sole of her boot, given time. Fire twisted beneath her skin, her furnace door flailing open. Deep down, she didn't want to run.

She wanted to fight. Gold-white smoke had taken Balthazar's eyes, but he still had a face, and she could claw it to ribbons. Her fingers craved it—to rip the skin, strip his muscle and sinew, reveal him for a flesh-and-blood human, and then less, to the bone, to nothing.

But he would only burn her skull from the inside out, the same as he'd done to Treasure. Her ashes would do no good. If Annette let him kill her now, she would never see Gloria again.

Sylvia scrambled up from the dirt behind him. She was supposed to run, too, and maybe the same stubbornness had taken them both, some new and terrible miracle pouring from Balthazar's face. She stretched to standing firm, and her eyepatch glared as bright as her eye.

"I want you to know something," she said. "My friend, the woman you killed? She was the only one of her. When we started together, she wanted her name to be

Resplendence. I told her she needed to pick a name these lushes could pronounce. So, she was Treasure. And you don't find Treasure twice."

She waited for a reaction. Balthazar gave none.

She flashed her teeth. "Do you understand? A friend like her only happens to you once."

Nothing. His non-eyes fixed on Annette. When he again wouldn't look Sylvia's way, she curled her lips and spat hard. It struck his face and sizzled steam.

His radiance swelled. He turned sneering at her, righteousness fuming in his chest.

"Not her!" Annette snapped, and she waved desperate hands for Sylvia to run.

Sylvia looked at her, frowning in regret. She had to see now—this was Annette. Not a monster. Just the same woman who'd shared a bed with her, and her late husband, and they knew enough about one another to destroy each other, and that had only made them cling harder.

They had to cling now, and not let this unholy preacher tear them apart. They'd lost too much tonight already.

"Eyes on me, Balthazar." Annette stamped the dirt, demanding Balthazar take notice. "This ain't about her, right? I'm the one you want, the one with the sickness."

His attention leaned Annette's way, and Sylvia loped out of the street, between another two houses. Her breath hitched at each step, the sobs giving way to panic, but this time Balthazar's head hardly twitched. Spit could be forgotten, but not his daughter's spreading infection.

He wanted Annette.

She would keep him wanting. One foot slid back, and she pretended to stumble. He started toward her, first a gentle step and then a longer stride. She retreated another step, another, eyes always on him, hopeful this was the right pace for Slim and Gloria to finish tinkering with their machine. There would be no going back once Balthazar rounded the saloon's corner on Annette's heels, so long as he hadn't caught and murdered her yet. She had to slow him down, had to make him *want* to take his time.

"What's your daughter's name?" she asked. "You keep demanding ours. Tell me hers."

A thin sheet of smoke rippled between Balthazar's severe lips as if he'd only sucked in a long cigar drag and held it, rather than billowed like a chimney from within. No words.

Annette's chest tightened. She was going to ruin this if she didn't think faster. "What did you do to her? I know it's your fault."

"There was no fault," Balthazar said. "I saved my daughter."

Annette broke eye contact for a two-second glance aside—traipsing backward past the late sheriff's empty house, still a ways to go—and then returned to Balthazar.

"What did you do?" she asked.

"I gave her everything, that's what I did!" he snapped. "But she mocked the scripture, broke the commandment to honor her father and mother. My wife saw nothing to this, but I witnessed a daughter damned." His steps slowed as his head eased over his neck, baring his throat. "But then great Gabriel offered salvation. No mother of God could descend into the abyss, no more than God Himself could be damned there. Do you understand? An immaculate conception."

"Yeah, I heard, heir to the Virgin Mary." Annette's next step faltered in earnest, and she hurried to right herself. Balthazar's catching up would mean the end. "But Mary could speak, couldn't she? People didn't sleepwalk in nightmares around her through Jerusalem, did they? Ain't ever heard in a church sermon about the time she cut out anyone's heart and intestines."

Somewhere beyond the street, a dry throat groaned with Saber's suffering, where she hopefully hadn't found Sylvia.

Annette puffed up her chest. "Tell me what you did, Balthazar."

A harsh squall pushed at her back and swept smoke from Balthazar's face. In the shimmer, his cheeks seemed damp. "My daughter refused the blessing."

"Refused," Annette echoed. "I take it your made-up angels didn't ask her?"

"Since when has asking mattered?" Balthazar raised a hand heavenward. "God's children must honor our glorious father."

Annette glanced aside—the cobbler's workshop. She pictured him dead inside, a leathery bald man lost in dreams when Saber crawled onto his and his wife's bed and cracked them open. Most people in Low's Bend had died in their sleep.

"You can't imagine," Balthazar said. "Heaven opened to me in a moment of sheer awe. Even holy men delude themselves with importance, I'm no better. Beneath that power, we are nothing. The angels told me to watch over my daughter, for she bore the Lord's return, and I would stand in His care." He glanced at his shoes and paused in the middle of the street. "But she wanted no part in it."

Right now he seemed more the man who'd sung of Mary and Joseph while playing the piano than he was the luminance coursing through him. Smoke and light felt no pain, but Balthazar looked hurt and ashamed.

Maybe there was no need for that ugly machine behind Slim's Respite. Annette could talk him down.

"What did she do, Balthazar?" she asked, forcing a calmer tone. "You can tell me."

Balthazar opened his mouth, shut it, opened it again. "She asked her mother to stop the Lord's return. Before His birth."

Annette slowed. "They were going to end it."

"I couldn't let them, and so I separated them." Balthazar took another step, and another, his confidence returning in heavy footfalls. "We planned to isolate ourselves, leave her mother behind if it meant saving my daughter's immortal soul. I would see to the coming of

Christ. Even then, she couldn't honor her father. First, she called on God to release her of this blessing. I let her make prayers and make peace, hoping the Lord would answer, or perhaps great Gabriel, who would tell her she had nothing to fear. I hoped she would at last understand."

Annette glanced right—the Smith house crawled by. To the left, another dry Saber-like groan.

"But when God didn't answer, she called to darker forces, begged all the devils in Hell to help her, and only then did I intervene." A white-hot sharpness slashed up Balthazar's chest. "The angels showed me how to protect her, even from herself. From then on, she would be as one immortal."

"And she spread it to me," Annette said. She thought of her quickly healing wound. Scarring too fast, but still raw. She had been hurt since Saber's passing the mark along. "But I ain't immortal. How do you know I'll turn out like her?"

"Because her mother nearly did." Balthazar's throat throbbed as if swallowing a painful memory. "When my daughter spread it to her, the mark paled my wife's skin, made her wrathful, drew her through nightmares to the Land of Nod. I ended her before the mark could take her beyond harm. She was too soft a mother to be a good woman anymore, and then too much an animal to let her roam free." A new frenzy flared in his eyes. "So, you see, I've sacrificed. And sacrificed. And I'll keep on sacrificing until the Lord's will is done."

A wave of the red nightmare washed across Annette's eyes. Frank lurched from his pool of blood and innards, his hand reaching out, black crust soiling the grooves of his fingertips. The copper smell dizzied her.

Not now, Frank. She couldn't go drowsy with Balthazar chasing. She pinched two soiled fingernails around her forearm's pale flesh, and the street faded in. Balthazar had gained ground in her fugue moment.

"How do I cure it?" Annette asked.

Smoke puffed thicker from Balthazar's eyes. "There is no unmaking this power. That is why the angels gave it. None will harm my daughter, not even herself. Her wrath will fall to others."

Annette plucked her fingernails up. Drops of blood now beaded from her skin. "I'm not like her."

"There is still time to hurt you, and end it, the way I ended her mother."

Balthazar's glow met the meager light of Slim's Respite and sent Annette's shadow dancing. She made a clumsy turn into the gap between the saloon and the Smith house.

"She prayed to the enemy!" Balthazar roared. "But I—I shouted her down. Shouted to the heavens!" His chest writhed, and his limbs and head jittered as if his bones meant to tear loose from his skin. "And. The angels. Answered!"

White light fountained up from his mouth, and its force knocked Annette to the ground.

"SHE. WILL. BE. MOTHER." Balthazar's jaw stretched wide, but he didn't sound like himself. A cluster of voices fought for space across the throat and tongue. "SHE. WILL. BE. HEIR."

Annette clawed at the dirt, trying to stand, but terror weighed her down, heavier than the world. He would catch her now. She'd saved Sylvia only to take her place.

The light recoiled into Balthazar's throat, and he seemed to swallow it. "With this destiny and the mark, she carries the strength of God's word and walks free of all harm, even her own." His head leaned toward Annette. "But then there's you."

She kicked scrambling backward until she staggered to her feet. Almost to the shed, almost done, she couldn't let him catch her now.

One steaming hand reached for her head. "I will not let her spread this mark," Balthazar said. His knees buckled, his steps were unsure. The light had spent him, but not enough to stop him. Ragged bits of flesh dripped through the smoke. "You will not follow her."

CRUEL ANGELS PAST SUNDOWN

Annette banged one shoulder against the back corner of Slim's Respite. Soil shifted underfoot. She had to be near enough to the shed, but she couldn't tear her eyes from Balthazar again. He had tossed wrongness in heaps onto her life, gleefully after having done it to himself and his unnamed wife and daughter.

Lost loved ones could make monsters of the survivors. Were someone to murder Gloria, Annette could see herself tossing her inner furnace door open. Frank's death had already put her brimming with fury. If she didn't reach the shed soon, that door would fly open. She would throw her rage onto Balthazar and kill herself failing to stop him.

A creaking moan sent a shudder down her spine. Saber must've somehow snuck behind her, leering, blade ready. She would cut Annette down, and then what would she do against Balthazar? He couldn't hurt her, but did she want to hurt him for everything he'd done? She should, if there were any thoughts left in her head.

A familiar whistle jerked Annette's gaze over her shoulder.

The creaking moan hadn't been Saber. It was the shed door's hinges as Gloria pressed it all the way open and filled the doorway. She had hands on her hips and her head cocked to one side, her hat's shadow hiding most of her face from Balthazar's light. Only her playful smirk glowed in the night.

Annette twisted into a mad dash for one side of the shed. She had to hope Gloria and Slim were ready.

Balthazar grimaced, and the light burned behind his teeth. "You again." The words came wet and sick as if it hurt to speak. He strode faster now.

"Closer, yes," Gloria whispered. "Come on, lad." She nodded at Annette and then slipped a step deeper into the shed, behind an iron shadow. Slim knelt at its side, his arms loaded with shining rounds.

"The gunslinger," Balthazar said, breath steaming. He reached one hand toward the shed, and a snake of light

107

writhed down his arm. Its radiance seeped through the shed's doorway and reflected off the metal shaft. "Tell me your name, child of God."

Gloria smirked again. "You can call me ma'am."

She aimed the long metal shaft and grasped a bent crank jutting from its side. The shaft turned, whined, and clapped thunder through the doorway like a stern hammer banging, banging, banging on a tin roof.

Annette jammed her hands over her ears, but the Gatling gun's tremor rocked through her anyway. Countless rounds, each a blinding flare in the night. Behind the flashing muzzle, Gloria shrieked some pent-up battle cry, the kind she might have shouted while driving her horse toward the worst men in the territory. A hailstorm of shells tore from the shed into Balthazar's glowing body.

The first rounds sent him jittering, and his light rushed through the new holes as if to mend them and fight back against the heedless thunder.

But the shells kept coming, and he stumbled backward, every part of him quaking. Gunfire chewed across his chest, legs, and head in a volley of hungry lead teeth, beating unmarred flesh into choppy ground meat. His ragged wounds burst into a slurry of crimson rain. Bits of bone shrapnel popped from his torso. Where skin and muscle sloughed away, gold-white light shined and then dimmed.

The Gatling gun hissed to a quieter clanging and then jerked to a stop. Slim's arms cradled empty air, and shell casings littered the earth.

Balthazar crumpled with them. On his knees, he reminded Annette of Treasure, and she wanted to tear after him, burn his skull out, lay him to ashes, and leave no trace of Balthazar Wilcox left in this world.

"He can't still be alive," Slim said, standing up. He sounded out of breath. "Damn near every round hit him. He should be red foam right now."

Gloria slid from behind the Gatling gun and emerged

from the shed. Her eyes stretched wide. "Don't you move, damn you," she whispered.

Balthazar floundered on jerking steps, unsure whether to keep living or start dying. His golden light thinned and yellowed through his bullet holes and dagger-made canyon, a radiant corpse who didn't know he was already dead. The wind gusted around the saloon and seemed to lift him. He was only loose parts now, stitched together by a memory of his former shape.

But he hadn't given up yet. He was standing, breathing. Walking. He might not catch anyone if they ran, but he wouldn't stop.

"The storm," Slim said. "We could hide in it." Light shimmered in a trickle of blood running down his cheek. Beside him, dark streaks rolled down Gloria's face.

A rumbling growl tore through Balthazar's approaching body. "Nowhere will hide you from the Lord's light," he said. His jaw hung slack from a chopped-up face.

Beneath him, another sound crept through the night.

Annette glanced past Gloria's and Slim's bloody faces, beyond Balthazar's stirring radiance, to the outer corner of Slim's Respite. Fingers of dust crept at wooden edges and cast a soiled veil across the window light.

A figure staggered closer, her shadow little more than a slit in the dirt.

Annette stiffened, understanding. The Gatling gun could only fight Balthazar's flesh. Whatever power he'd drawn up lived inside him, something he called godly, and nothing Slim pulled out of his shed measured up to that mighty force.

But a command of God might. Or a curse. At least, if Balthazar was right about the mark and its source.

Annette skirted around Gloria and Slim, closer to the saloon. "Stop me," she said. "Don't let me end up like your daughter. Someone you can't hurt."

Balthazar turned, his face a cavern of light. What features remained had been beaten into dangling tendrils of meat. He lurched toward Annette in clumsy steps. The ragged remains of a chewed-up hand stretched after her.

She dodged toward the corner. Her sight ran red, the nightmare coming as if Balthazar had smeared his pulpy fingers across her eyes, but she couldn't stop yet. The air grew heavy with debris, and floating sediment pinched her eyes. A moan tore beside her.

"Come to me," Balthazar said. "I will help you, child of God."

"But who will help you?" Annette asked. She retreated one last step and let him reach the wooden corner and its creaking voice.

Coming face to no-face with his daughter. Dust clung to the bloody splotches patterning her bony legs. Her dull eyes seemed to find him through her inner haze.

The light trembled in his skull. A red sheen tangled with the billowing dust. Balthazar's hanging jaw dripped, and another growl slithered up his throat, maybe to shout Saber down, or say her true name, or pray she let him be.

Her sword plunged under his cavernous sternum and found what remained of his lungs, his heart. She reached her free hand past his outstretched arm and dug into his lit-up head. Curling fingers clawed dark slush down the gaping spaces where his nose and lips used to be, and the light flickered in their wake. The radiance that had burned Treasure would not stop Saber. It shrank beneath the protective power in her marked skin, wavering and helpless as she tore a damp lump loose from Balthazar's skull. Something important. Something the light needed.

His jellying legs sent him reeling backward. His radiance began to fade in a billowing cloud. Had the storm wrapped him in sand, or was he finally going to die?

"You cannot stop the coming of the Lord." His words climbed smothered and damp as if drowning inside him. Whatever power had let his voice flow without vocal cords now sounded weak and uncertain. He would lose his speech soon, and then everything else. He faded from sight, cavalry saber still jutting from his gut, but his ragged voice bellowed in the gale. "For the wages of sin is death, but the gift of God is eternal life in Christ Jesus, our Lord."

Saber curled a fist and lowered it to her side. Another moan ebbed up her throat in halting bursts, a kind of weep-croaking Annette had never heard before. It made her cringe and tear up at once. Saber fell to the dirt, and the storm surrounded her.

If Annette let her fury loose to throttle Saber, the red nightmare would smother every thought like before. Only Frank would fill her thoughts. Much as she wanted, this fight would be pointless.

Balthazar had no such protection. And deep down, was it truly Saber's fault she had come to the ranch in the first place? She and her sword had killed Frank, but had she been the one to wield it when her fury and the nightmare drove her on?

Exactly who had burdened her with this misery? Who deserved to pay? Deserved Annette's revenge?

She slung an arm over her eyes to block the wind and then slipped around Saber. Ahead, a darkening shape made for the far side of Slim's Respite, a steel blade sticking from his back. Where would he go now? What did he have left to call into him?

Another figure reached Annette's side. She almost darted back in case Saber had decided to chase, but this figure looked nothing like Saber.

"Don't come with me," Annette said. "Please."

"We've gone this far," Gloria said. She coughed and spat, struggling to speak without the wind blowing debris into her mouth. "I won't let him go to ground and play some other odd trick. He'll hunt us again, you watch."

Not us, Annette almost said. *Me.* She wanted Gloria and Slim to hunker down in the shed, or inside the saloon with the shutters up. They didn't have to chase Balthazar. They didn't have to find out if he knew a cure for the mark, a secret he might give up with his dying breath.

Annette pursed her lips and strode deeper into the dusty onslaught. If that celestial eye wreathed in writing watched her, she couldn't see it through the storm. That didn't mean it had closed itself to Balthazar entirely. Having Gloria with her would at least make the unknown a little less terrifying.

"So, we fix our eyes not on what is seen," Balthazar said, "but on what is unseen, since what is seen is temporary, but what is unseen is eternal."

Bible passages. Almost like witches' spells for him. He was up to something more. Annette and Gloria passed the far corner of Slim's Respite and followed Balthazar's faint shape up alongside the building, toward another wooden wall and doorway.

"The stables," Gloria said, voice rising and falling in the blinding gale. She grasped Annette's hand as dust veiled her face. Annette could hardly see her anymore.

New sounds joined the airy cacophony—whinnying horses, a lowing bull. Balthazar had kicked open the stable doors and let the dust storm join the animals. One horse screamed, and Annette could have lived a better life had she never heard that pleading cry. Big Pete nearly roared. What was Balthazar doing to them? He'd vanished from sight, a ghost in the debris.

Only his voice haunted the air. "The world and its desires pass away."

Annette charged onward, pulling Gloria. "Balthazar, stop!"

The stable walls should have kept out some of the storm, but the soil would not relent. Flailing darkness batted at Annette's sight. Balthazar had to be right ahead of her, so loud and righteous.

"But whoever does the will of God—"

The wind quit blowing and instead yanked hard. Annette flung forward, dragging Gloria. They were careening into Balthazar's words as if he were drawing them down his throat.

"—lives forever."

Splinters cracked from the walls. The horses and bull shifted heavily against the earth, the sky thundered, and Annette lost all sight. This place was only angry dust and howling darkness. The back wall had to have shattered; they had walked too far. They should have come out the other end by now.

"Annette?" Gloria cried like a distant echo. She had fallen down some deep pit, and Annette with her, but they had strayed apart. The tempest was a mountain between them.

And then its gusty mountain crumbled. Annette's ears popped, and she thought they might be bleeding. Both hands tightened—one into a fist, the other answering Gloria's grasp. The storm bowed beneath them. The end was coming, and Annette could only hope Balthazar suffered whatever she and Gloria were about to suffer.

The dust vanished, and the world went white.

FIFTEEN:
THE PLAINS

ANNETTE STEPPED FROM what should have been the back of the stables into still air and blinding daylight. Her eyelids narrowed as she thrust her arm to her forehead, but she had to blink again and again before she could see past her nose.

Even then, what she saw didn't make sense. No familiar bush-dotted prairie lay before her. She couldn't make out Slim's shed, the saloon, or anything else she knew.

A wide white plain stretched to the horizon, topped nearby with pale rocky pillars and distantly with the vast behemoths of flat-roofed mesas. Sharp golden sunshine burned down stagnant air, cooking the sand as pale as Annette's marked skin. The soil stretched dry and scaly, cracking in places like a thirsty man's chapped lips.

Echoing footsteps bounded across the ivory desert, and Annette realized she was still walking. She forced herself to stop. Another set of footsteps mimicked hers and then halted beside her.

Gloria was here. The stables stood behind her, and some of the animals remained inside. Where the rest had gone was a mystery, but those few present had calmed since the storm's vanishing. Night had turned to day in the time since Annette and Gloria crossed the stables from the entrance to the end. A back wall should have stopped them, but now it was gone and what lay beyond was changed.

CRUEL ANGELS PAST SUNDOWN

Low's Bend did not surround the stables. The town was gone, replaced by the endless white plain. Parched earth reached the horizon in every direction, shaded only where the rocks and mesas stood defiant against the sunshine.

"I don't understand," Gloria said. Her hat shielded her face, but the pale earth reflected sunlight almost as harshly as snow, and even from her brim's shadow, she had to squint to see.

Annette touched the nearest wooden wall—solid, real. The inside smelled of hay and animal hair, and it reminded her of Frank and the ranch. Better to put those memories aside; her troubles right now were more immediate. The stables had followed her and Gloria, but the rest of town hadn't made the journey.

To where?

Annette stepped inside to give her eyes a rest from the sun. She passed the horses, Big Pete, and reached the entrance where Balthazar had thrust open the doors. She should have found the rough street of Low's Bend, its earth beaten by boots and horse hooves. Looking left should have shown her the porch of Slim's Respite—instead, there lay the desert. And across the non-street, the house whose residents she'd forgotten—desert—and beside it, Arch's house—more desert.

She crossed the threshold. If she had come to this dry place through the back of the stables, stepping out the main doorway should show her the town.

There was only daylight, only this wasteland. Whatever magic trick had sent her, Gloria, and the animals here, it would not buckle inward and return them to the world they knew. The entrance was no secret doorway. Some fundamental truth about the world had twisted night to day, home to a strange land.

This was Balthazar's Christly witchcraft again. Annette couldn't explain any better than that. She returned to Gloria, who hadn't moved.

"I don't understand," she said again. Her accent sounded thick, her tongue parched.

HAILEY PIPER

The sunlight weighed on Annette's head, and she swayed briefly into the red nightmare, its dampness almost a relief against the desert. Frank's face filled her sight, and she fought her head out again from red to white, two flavors of hellishness she didn't understand.

Was this emptiness a dream, too? Annette wanted to think so, but nightmares were lonely places, and she wasn't alone.

She reached out for Gloria. Her duster's sleeve creased, the arm beneath thick and firm. She shrugged Annette off, crouched to the earth, and scooped up a handful of white sand. Her lips moved, and though she didn't make a sound, Annette thought they curved in a circle, then curled back from teeth, and then opened in a now-familiar phrase. *I don't understand.*

"Balthazar," Annette said. "It couldn't have been Saber. He did this."

There was no telling which parts of his rambling were desperate sermons and which were bizarre magic dredged up from holy scripture, but he had been conjuring to draw the light inside him. Now he'd torn a hole in the world.

Annette scanned the horizon for any sign of dwellings, trails, or people. Natural formations filled the world. Nothing else.

"If we climb high up, we might spot a town," she said. "A road we can follow, I don't know. It would be something, at least."

Gloria didn't look at Annette. She seemed fixed on her palm, where dry earth would soon turn skin to scales.

Annette reached for Gloria's arm again. "We'll have better luck finding anyone to tell us where we are. Ain't likely to figure it out standing here."

"Haven't we figured it out?" Gloria let white sand sift through her fingers. "I think we know exactly where we are." No wind batted at the falling grains, as if the dust storm in Low's Bend had used up every last gust in the world. "Don't you?"

"I thought you didn't understand." Annette felt it, though. Balthazar had droned on enough about it tonight—last night? She had taken his words for hollow preacher talk, becoming real only when she couldn't ignore what shined in front of her face. Men like him loved to hear themselves speak, loved to pretend they guarded the gateway to souls' destinies.

Gloria's hand curled into a fist. "Where else would that man bring us?"

He had been charged with radiance even in his mangled state. Carved open by his own crucifix-dagger, beaten pulpy by the Gatling gun, and then broken inside somehow by his daughter's eternal hand. The light had felt so empty and absent. Maybe that was why whatever strange eye Annette had seen watching before the storm had decided to keep its distance, closed its eyelid to hide, and never touched Low's Bend. It didn't want to be tainted.

Gloria at last looked up. "You understand, Butterfly," she said. "I do, too."

Annette did. Not because she wanted to, but because she couldn't escape it. She thought of Treasure kneeling in the street. Of Balthazar's merciless hand, his cruel lips and tongue.

"The absence of God," Annette recited. "Hell awaits."

SIXTEEN:
A LAND OF PAIN

GLORIA TREADED TOWARD the blasted earth, catching its cracks in her intense stare. Debris from the Low's Bend storm filled the folds of denim at her thighs, but it paled in the sunshine.

Annette couldn't read her. She could hardly read herself. The earth felt firm, the world solid and yet dreamlike and unbelievable. They shouldn't have come striding into the stables. And if they'd had no choice but to come here, at the least they should have found Balthazar outside with them. He had only been staggering a few feet ahead.

But what did distance matter here?

"Markings, aren't they?" Gloria muttered. Her boot toed at one crack in the ground.

Annette leaned down for a closer look. Rounded grooves marred the white soil along one black line, sliding one way to a point, and then another, and so on as far as she could see. These were the footprints of someone walking these crooked roads.

Which way was ahead? The back of the stables had aimed west from Low's Bend, but did direction matter outside the world? Was there a north in Hell?

The questions hurt Annette's head. Balthazar was the one who'd opened the way, and he had walked here. No one else could have made these tracks.

"He went this way." Annette's dress pulled at her, its bloody left side crusting over in the baked air. "He stood right where we stand and started walking. We could find him."

Gloria scanned the footprints up and down. Her experience at tracking elusive men had helped her spot them against this desolate landscape, but she showed no compulsion to follow. Her body seemed to sag inside her clothes. They had to be hot and weighing on her.

"He led us here," Annette said. "He could lead us out." She reached for Gloria's hand and squeezed.

Gloria squeezed back with a sigh. "Balthazar or not, we've quite little else to go on." She drew Annette close. "I want you to wait for me here. Don't come fluttering after me for once. You're unwell. I'll come back when I find the way."

Annette dipped her face beneath the brim of Gloria's hat. "I'm going with you."

"You're not yourself," Gloria said. She held up Annette's hand. "You're in no fit condition to hunt men across the desert."

"I might never be fit again," Annette said.

The sun had dried any remaining gore from her hand, and now patches of too-white skin broke through the flaking crimson. Its scales echoed the wasteland up to the wrist, where her complexion caught Hell's sunshine, nearly white as the sand. The pale mark hadn't killed her, but it had ruined some crucial part of her and might ravage her worse.

If she was sick with it, would always be sick with it, then it wasn't as if hunting Balthazar for starting this chaos would make it any worse. She had no reason to let him go. If she could open the furnace door inside her on purpose, she would do it for him. Throw the preacher in with the fire.

She looked into Gloria's eyes. "I'm going with you."

Gloria stared, softened, and then nodded.

Opening the stables and readying her white gelding,

Salt, with saddle and reins only took a few minutes—or, was time real here? Annette tried not to think about it. She had enough trouble deciding on a horse before ultimately drawing Big Pete out onto the cracked earth. No saddle would fit him, but he was the only animal here besides Salt that Annette trusted, and in this oppressive atmosphere, she didn't want to overburden one beast with two riders.

On any ordinary day, Gloria would have protested, or at least given Annette a queer look for climbing onto a bull's back, even one as lethargic as Big Pete. She said nothing now. She wouldn't break her stare from Balthazar's tracks, as if the scaly earth would swallow them should she glance away.

They kept a slow but steady pace over the sun-battered landscape. Balthazar's footprints sometimes left the black lines to walk in a mesa's shade, and the shadows' angles never changed. Even after riding Salt and Big Pete far enough that Annette couldn't see the stables when she glanced back, the shadows remained where Balthazar had stepped through them. Nothing changed here, and the golden glow above seemed to swirl in place. It might not have been a sun at all, but Annette couldn't imagine what else might glow across the sky.

Atop a faraway mesa, shadows writhed as if cast by flickering candlelight. They looked formless at first, and Annette could believe they were shades of the red nightmare, trying new tricks to get her attention.

But the shadows climbed jagged rock across the mesa's plateau and twisted into clearer shapes with firmer forms. Wild thrashing heads, four legs, flailing manes, a silent stampede of darkness in the daylight. If this was a memory, it wasn't Annette's, but she saw it just the same.

"Look at them," she said.

Gloria lifted her heavy head and fixed on the distant mesa. A sharp breath slid through her lips.

"See the horses?" Annette pointed to the shadows. "Are they alive?"

"What horses?" Gloria asked.

Annette watched the galloping shadows to be certain they weren't odd goats or deer—no, they were horses—and then looked to Gloria. Her eyes held wide, and her face formed a circle of stunned horror.

"You don't see horses?" Annette asked. "What do you see then?"

Gloria half-lidded her gaze at Salt's fair mane. "You wouldn't understand."

Annette glanced at the mesa, but the shadow play was dissolving. She could imagine dust motes from the unreal horses' hooves, but within a few blinks, the mirage went still and no horses remained.

Except for Salt. He kept even with Big Pete, never pressing ahead. He seemed rested, but the steady pace wasn't for the horse's benefit. Gloria's every breath strained as if she were trying to move a mountain.

She would shed red tears again soon. They had left Saber in Low's Bend, but Annette's sickness would soon worsen, exactly as Balthazar had said. First, the people around her would feel drowsiness, then they would bleed from their eyes. Soon she would sink again into her own crimson dreamland, maybe forever this time.

Frank stared through the back of her mind. What did he want? She couldn't undo his death. Was he here to punish her? To hear her confess to secrets and beg forgiveness? Her throat was scratchy from sucking in cooked air. She imagined her speech would soon collapse into creaking groans.

There might be little time left with Gloria.

Finding Balthazar had a chance of returning them to the world if they were lucky, but it would not cure this pale mark coating Annette's body. Soon, she would wander. After that, she might kill.

"Remember when I first got that scar on my arm, from burning it on the pan?" she asked, and watched Gloria's head bob with Salt's sway. "I showed it to you the next time you came to Low's Bend and said I wanted to lie about where it came from, tell folk I'd ridden down a murderer like I was you. Like I could do what you do. And you told me, 'Be proud of yourself. You keep bellies full, it's honorable work.' You said what these hands do matters."

Her paraphrasing sounded haughtier than she meant, but she hoped to see a smirk on Gloria's face, some acknowledgment of this terrible impression of her accent. Maybe some of Frank's humor had bled into Annette in the end.

Gloria sat expressionless.

Annette glanced over Big Pete's horns, where the white wastes looked no different ahead than behind. She raised her arm and examined the skin below the wrist. "Can't even see the scar now, the skin's turned so—" A hoarse crackle cut her off. She rubbed at her throat and hoped for rain. As if a little water might cure the pale mark.

Salt began to wander from the trail, and Gloria either didn't notice or didn't care. Her head lolled over his mane, her stare burning through his hide.

She wasn't drowsy from Annette's sickness. This was despair. Annette had seen moods of this nature when Gloria was homesick, not because she held any strong love for England, but sometimes she missed the damp gray familiarity, aspects of the past that told her life had been simpler before she came chasing a wilder fate on the American frontier. There was comfort in an absent home.

"Salt," Annette said.

The horse's ears twitched. She clicked her tongue to draw him closer. It felt fat in the back of her mouth as if it would soon unroll and taste the not-sunshine. Gloria's horse didn't need to know that. There was no steering Big Pete, he marched with the guidance of his own bovine compass, but Salt knew Annette and could be brought back to the path.

She clicked her tongue again. "Salt, here."

His ears twitched, and he trotted nearby with a soft

whinny. Gloria shuffled but said nothing. Her arms squeezed her sides, hands pressed together in front of her chest. She seemed desperate to curl up into herself. The sun here didn't warm, but the air wasn't cold, either. Nothing significant in this place but its sheer vastness, and the desert did not seem eager to make any impression besides echoes and shadows. It lay around them, unaffecting and apathetic. Endless, careless nothingness.

"I bet this is how you look chasing bounties," Annette said. "Gloria and Salt against the big open world."

She didn't mean it. She had always pictured Gloria the way she'd stormed into the saloon to stop Balthazar, her duster whipping in the wind, gridiron hot in her hand. Not slumped over Salt's saddle horn, reins tucked loosely between her fingers and palms.

Maybe Annette's imagination expected too much. Maybe Gloria never liked riding off from Low's Bend. She might have grown tired and wanted to settle down, be done with everything.

Now wasn't the time, not in this desolation. They had to keep on.

"This chase ain't so different from your usual," Annette said. "Balthazar's your mark. The bounty is going home. We can work like that."

Gloria's brow furrowed. "What if there is no going home?"

"There is." Annette ran her hand down Big Pete's coarse-haired neck. "He led us here, remember? He can lead us back."

Gloria at last turned her head, heavy as a boulder. "If we're cold and hungry, do we live? Do our footsteps feel the earth? Do we still wear skin? If we're stuck in Hell, alive—what does that mean for our flesh? Our souls?"

Annette didn't have answers. Balthazar might. She glanced again past Big Pete's head and eyed the black-lined earth for smudges and tracks. They were keeping to Balthazar's trail.

"You ran off again." There was an accusatory note in Gloria's voice; nothing good would come of what she said next.

Annette forced her eyes to one side, tracing Salt's white hide and then Gloria's pinched expression. Her mood was darker than Annette had realized.

"After Treasure—God rest her soul—told me of your battling that man in Slim's, I asked if you meant to keep this special union we have," Gloria said, terse and scathing. "And you told me you were sorry. I believed you. But then you bloody chased after him, again and again, like you've got a death wish, like you don't—like you're eager to join your Frank."

"I'm not," Annette said, desperate. Red flashed behind her eyes. If only Gloria knew how close Frank could sit beyond death.

"But that isn't my way." Gloria swallowed hard. "I don't have a death wish."

"I ain't asking that for you." Annette lowered her head. "Everything went lightning fast in the night. Maybe something in me thought I was being brave, like you."

"Annette," Gloria said, her voice forcing patience. "I've a life. I want to live it. I wasn't looking to hunt and hunt until one day some cutthroat, with more friends than the wanted poster told about, guns me down and leaves me for dead. I crossed the Atlantic on a daring lie. I'll wager that sounds romantic to you, isn't that right? You have me painted as this roaming adventurer in your head, some folk hero whose story might sweep you from the ranch life, but the truth is, no matter what anyone says, I need peace someday. I need softness, comfort, and love. Even if I have to pretend we're spinsters, I want those things."

Annette glanced between Salt and Big Pete, and then she reached for Gloria's hand.

Gloria clutched Salt's reins and didn't let go. "Can you give me that peace? Can you give me any of it? You had no plans to do so before, and I deserve better than your fluttering and fawning."

"I ain't understanding you." Annette's throat tightened. "I'm right here."

"You didn't choose between me or Frank. You wanted everything, but now he's dead." Gloria eased back in her saddle and gave a slow nod. "Of course, how can I blame you? I want it all, too. Frank's gone, and you want revenge, but I'm not your oblivious husband. I see through you."

The redness tugged Annette's thoughts, but she reeled forward. "Tell me what you mean," she said, hand still outstretched, as if Gloria might pull her from an evil dream. "I loved him. I love you."

"There was a time you loved us both, alive. It wasn't long ago, and I never meant to be selfish." Gloria shook her head, moving her hat's shadow back and forth over her face. "He and I might have been mates at some time. We might have sorted all this out, but there's no plain solution anymore. The poor man's dead. And I for one believe I deserve better than your throwing yourself my way the moment your heart is no longer torn in two."

Annette let her hand fall to her side. "You're right."

Gloria bristled like she hadn't expected to hear that. "Ann—"

"No, you're right. It ain't fair of me, like I could go running from the guilt over him into your arms. Like you hadn't been kept to the side. You deserve better. You deserve everything, and I tried to pretend life could go on this way forever like we'd never age. I didn't know what else to do, and I loved him, and I love you, and I'm sorry. You're right."

Gloria glanced at Annette's lowered hand and then back to her eyes. "Does being right mean anything here?"

Annette wasn't sure it had to mean anything, anywhere. What mattered most was what they wanted.

She watched pillars of rock slide past. Hell held no hills or proper mountains, only the bulky formations and the distant impression of a thickening sky. Some monstrous terrain might stand beyond sight, but Annette couldn't be sure. Her eyes were tired.

She and Gloria brought the animals to rest in the shadow of a stunted mesa. With the not-sun fixed in place, there was no telling how much time has passed, but the night had been long already, and no one had eaten or drank much in the meantime. They each ate a little jerky from Salt's pack and put the rest aside for when they'd need it later. Gloria passed a skin of water between herself and Annette, and then she poured water into her cupped hand and let Salt and Big Pete lap up their share. Annette wished she'd found a way to take some from the stable buckets, but the horses there needed to drink too.

Gloria unrolled a rough hide from Salt's saddle and spread it along the mesa's foundation where Annette had kicked a clearing free of small stones. She sat down first and offered her arms to Gloria. The despair haunted Gloria's face as if she might sink into shadow and vanish, but Annette could look desperate, too, and Gloria relented.

Annette was not soft. She had known this since first touching Treasure and later Sylvia long ago. Their skin hadn't been leathery like Annette's, their muscles not drawn tight and sinewy by ranch work and a merciless sun. They worked in other ways.

Gloria had never complained when she eased into bed and invited Annette to join her. She didn't complain now as her head rested on Annette's chest. The peace and softness she needed ran deeper than flesh and bone, down to touch and soul. Even in Hell.

She held Gloria's shoulders, pressed her hat away, and kissed her head. They could stay like this, Annette giving Gloria at least a fragment of what she deserved, until the mark's sickness took over and some version of Frank would rule the red nightmare. In the wasteland's stillness, the infection might take its time.

Annette leaned down to kiss Gloria's hair again and found Gloria's face peering up instead. The mesa's shadow thickened around them, and then their lips touched and opened. Annette felt a hand at her chest, crossing from wounded to unwounded side, and a throbbing stirred deep beneath her skin and scar tissue.

Her brow furrowed. "Now?"

"When else would we have?" Gloria asked.

She was right. Annette leaned into another, deeper kiss. Heaviness drew dark curtains in her head, but she never sank into the nightmare. Always she felt the stiff air, and warm breath, and she remembered where to find Gloria's scars beneath her clothes and kiss them as if her lips could heal. Gloria reached through the tear in Annette's dress and traced the wound across her breast, mended to a thin grimace. Their clothes began to shed beneath their fingers.

This world was a wide-open place, but they pressed into the mesa, and it seemed to hold them. Gloria ran hands down Annette's sides, stirring the trembling places across her body. Annette kissed Gloria's tender forearms, her round belly, her soft thigh, and then Annette hovered over a patch curling hair and kissed between warm thighs, too. Gloria found Annette's messy hair and coiled her fingers through it, each tip tracing the contours of Annette's skull.

Drinking in shadow, and each other, there was no nightmare, no dry throat, no sign of the mark until Annette curled an arm around each of Gloria's thighs and poured her overlong tongue into damp sweetness. The snaking tissue should have alarmed her, but she let it guide her up soft lips and deeper tastes. There was no point stopping, and all the reason to press into Gloria's tensing form. Annette would give, and love, and try to think of nothing else.

She only wondered if this was the first time anyone had screamed pleasure in this endless land of pain.

When they were worn out and soaked in sweat, they curled into each other against the mesa's foot. Annette let the heaviness take her while she listened to hooves scrape the earth. In her dreams, she worried she would see devils instead of Salt and Big Pete, but her sleep was peaceful and as full of Gloria as waking life.

There was no one to judge here. No reason to hide, or make excuses, or pretend Annette wanted nothing more than to hear about Gloria's travels. No secrets. Hell kept a kind of peace in that way, a quiet Annette had never known. She slept harder here than she could remember anywhere else.

When she woke up, Gloria was gone.

SEVENTEEN:
A LONELY PLACE

ANNETTE CALLED OUT into the desert. Gloria's name echoed in waves, several faraway Annette-like throats having likewise misplaced the woman she loved. If vague mesas could hear the call, Gloria had to hear, too.

Her clothes were gone. Salt, as well. She might have led him around the mesa. There were no tracks, but Annette had to look and hope the desert had the power to give Gloria back.

She followed the steep foundation, first through its shadow, and then out of it and around the base. The unremarkable landscape made her worry she might lose direction, but the mesa was small, and she kept a hand patting its side so she would not stray.

She was sweating again by the time the black shape of Big Pete appeared again in the shade. She slumped to the earth beside him and hoped to see Gloria's silhouette approach from one end of the desert or another.

Waiting would have been easier if the not-sun ever moved. The shadows should be crawling, and every mesa and rock pillar should become a natural sundial. Annette could have guessed an hour's passing, a day. Some sign that time would pass in the wasteland.

The not-sun only spun in place, eternal and unchanging in its mad little circle. Annette surrendered to counting the seconds under her breath, with no promises of accuracy. Every time she reached a minute, she scratched a line in the soil.

At fifty lines, she decided Gloria wasn't coming back.

Had another dust storm blown through while they slept? The last one had swallowed them into this desert; another might have swept Gloria back to Low's Bend and left Annette behind. She doubted it. They had been clutching each other tight, and a storm couldn't explain the disappearance of Gloria's clothes, or why Salt had vanished but not Big Pete.

Hell is a lonely place, Balthazar had said.

Annette forced herself to search the zigzagging crags beyond the mesa's shadow. Had Gloria never pointed out the grooves in the earth, Annette wouldn't have spotted them or known to follow, but now she recognized the impressions heel to toe on sight.

Balthazar's trail.

Had Gloria followed him on her own? She'd been pressed to leave Annette behind at the stables, but to abandon her in the middle of the desert seemed cruel. Besides, there were no adjacent tracks for Gloria's boots, no hoofprints by Salt. Where was the horse?

Annette looked at Big Pete. "Maybe Salt grew wings, and Gloria rode him to the sky."

Big Pete stamped at the earth and huffed dust across Balthazar's nearest footprint. No other tracks in sight, nothing else to go on.

Annette could only follow the awkward trail and hope to find Gloria somewhere along the way. She might have hidden her tracks, and Salt's too. She would know how to do that in ways neither Annette nor Balthazar could imagine.

Annette stood wearily beside Big Pete and rubbed his side. He felt sturdy, as if he could march another thousand miles, but with Salt gone, there was no more water. Forcing Big Pete onward didn't feel right, and if he went at all, she wouldn't make him bear her.

CRUEL ANGELS PAST SUNDOWN

He turned his large dark eyes her way. They held a calmer world, one where sunset fell like usual and brought all sleepers into easy dreams.

Annette scratched beside his neck. "If you know something I don't, you would tell me, right?"

Big Pete huffed again, likely relieved to stand out in the sun without a swarm of flies chewing him down. He looked to Balthazar's tracks.

"Sure, sure, you make a fair point." Annette scratched him another moment and then turned to follow the awkward trail. At every step, Big Pete's hooves patted the ground behind her.

Nothing else made a noise. On the most lonesome stretches of prairie, there were the sounds of insects and birds and wind, but the wasteland gave only echoes. Annette called for Gloria, and her own voice answered between mid-mesa canyons and arching rock formations. The rest of this world lay desperate or dead.

It reminded her of Saber. She had a thirst, and a hunger, every part of her quaking with a need to lose her unborn child, living in her alongside whatever fury came with the mark.

The red nightmare stroked the edges of Annette's sight, offering a deep lake where she could drown her thoughts. Frank's face appeared, and she thought the absence of noise in this wasteland let her at last hear his voice. Calling to her. Blaming her.

"Get out of my head," she muttered.

Let me out of your head, she thought he might have whispered, but it was likely a distorted echo. Frank never had a vengeful bone in his body. How much wrong had she done to him that he would haunt her now?

Fine, she should've been honest about never wanting children, should've shouted for help in the night, fought against Saber, done anything of use. No matter the rest though, he had loved her, and she still loved him.

She could open the furnace door inside and let its fire

slip past her memories and through her body. The desert offered little for it to harm. If she lashed out against stone and earth, it wasn't like anyone would care. Even Gloria couldn't chastise over it. And where the hell had she gone?

"Gloria!"

Annette called and called until her echoes sent chills down her spine. With no one real to talk to, they were beginning to sound like other people mocking her, and she would rather walk in silence than listen to warped waves of *Gloria-Gloria-ia-a-a!*

Shapes slithered in the distance, the mesas dancing a new waltz of shadows atop their plateaus. As Balthazar's trail led toward a wall of smooth rock, the shadows over one pillar took on crisp forms, and two of them climbed from the earth.

They were men. Brothers. One shadow hollowed with open fire inside him; the other blocked his inner fire with a mound of earth. They began to quarrel, and the fire-hearted brother lifted the shadow of a stone as big as his chest and smashed it over the earth-hearted brother's skull. Crimson life spattered both brothers and the white mesa beneath them. The murdered shadow fell and joined the earth. The murderous shadow burned pale and became one with the chalky desolation, his skin ashen, and then the figures vanished.

Annette stared for what felt like a long while to see if they would return. They did not. She opened her mouth to call out, but she didn't think anyone would hear. No one had stood on that mesa. The shadows were another echo, not of Gloria's name, but of something else.

She had an idea now of who might have first carried the pale mark and burned fiery inside, and perhaps passed some of both traits down to his children. It trickled to their children, too, and their children, spreading like a widening puddle, wet everywhere but never deep in one place. Never so potent again.

Until the mark came to Saber.

CRUEL ANGELS PAST SUNDOWN

Annette scanned the cracked soil for stones. There were pebbles, but nothing like the brutal rock the fire-hearted shadow had wielded. She wondered about trying to hurt herself with such a stone, if that would break her from this place to the Frank in her head. When Saber had tried harming herself, the red nightmare had dragged her down. Was Annette's mark that far gone already?

The fire inside didn't want her to hurt herself anyway. It had been burning all her life, and it wanted out. She would nurture this rage if she had nothing else. It wouldn't help her find Gloria or escape this place, but its uselessness in the greater scheme of Annette's life didn't mean it was done with her.

Another shadow play began atop a neighboring mesa. This time, Annette knew the figures—one was Gloria, the other Frank. They did not quarrel like the brothers. Gloria tipped her hat, and Frank tipped his. This was some meeting about the one whose heart split in two between them. Gloria threw her head back in laughter, and Frank spoke with his hands, and they came to a mutual agreement that Annette was a creature of some difficulty.

In the end, they shook hands and stepped away. The shadows melted into the mesa as if they had never risen.

Annette wondered if this, too, had ever happened. An echo of some commiseration between the people she loved most, some secret meeting while she slept or visited town. If this was true, both her closest lovers had put themselves through too much trouble for her.

But now Gloria was lost, and Annette had let Frank die. Like he didn't matter, like she didn't love him. He might have died thinking that, the idea smothered somewhere in the Saber-driven drowsiness. Annette hadn't realized the truth while chatting in Slim's Respite, running around Low's Bend, or traveling beside Gloria through this wasteland, but alone with Big Pete and the wind, Annette found no escaping it.

She deserved to be haunted. That was why Frank lingered in her head. Why he always would.

Shadows again danced distantly. If she didn't get moving, another play would begin, and she would stand forever watching worldly echoes, never finding Balthazar or the real Gloria.

Annette hurried on, leading Big Pete along and wrestling with the furnace door within. Her fingers twitched at her sides. If she were one of the brothers in the earlier shadow play, she would not have been the one to pour soil over his fire and then die. She would have been the brother who lifted the stone. Her fire would have given strength and kept her going as far as she needed, around this rock face, through a canyon, out across the endless vastness of Hell, for all eternity if that was how long it took her to find a way.

She wondered if the dead brother had haunted his murderous sibling the way Frank sat in a gory pool in her head. Sometimes crawling and reaching. Always staring. Maybe whispering, or suggesting a whisper, which was worse. She wondered if the murderous brother had come to hate and fear his victim.

As she emerged from the canyon, her attention slid from the inner furnace door and red nightmare to a gargantuan form ahead.

The mesas she had passed already were mere children to this tremendous grandfather. A calcified behemoth swelled before her, white as bone. Its shadow stretched to one side and swallowed other mesas beneath it. A crack down the center formed a towering black slit, small to the mesa itself, but wider than two wagons set side by side. It would someday sever the plateau above and split the mesa's core into a massive ravine.

At its foot, there walked a still-darker figure, draped in preacher's clothes. No white light poured from his chest, and his jacket and pants were whole and unbloodied, but he was the same man who'd stabbed Annette outside her ranch house, slashed himself from groin to throat in Slim's Respite, and poured a heavenly nightmare across Low's Bend.

"Balthazar," Annette said, and she tasted blood—her dry lips had split open.

Her throat crackled, and she lost her fight with the fire. Its furnace door slammed open with a heavy roar.

She didn't mind. There was no one to keep safe in this wasteland, no one to distract her. No reason to tamp down the fire or battle the door again. She didn't care if the fury couldn't help her escape. It could help in other ways.

It could hurt *him*.

She dashed from Big Pete, shrieking wild across the white-dust plain, as Balthazar glanced over his shoulder. His face was healed. He cut a black-lined smile, tipped his hat, and vanished into the mesa's ravine.

This had to be a trap. Annette couldn't guess why or how, her thoughts were burning too fast, but she knew he could have kept ahead of her if he wanted. He had been waiting.

She didn't care. He had waited, and she had caught up, and he would regret it the moment he felt her touch. She reached the mesa's foot and chased him inside the ravine.

Did she deserve to be haunted? That was fine. Everyone would get what was coming to them.

And Balthazar deserved to die.

EIGHTEEN:
TO THE SKY

BOTH INNER SIDES of the giant mesa's canyon sprouted jagged outcroppings and formed clumsy narrow paths where they hadn't yet broken apart. Slanted spokes of pale light rained down the gloomy canyon, sometimes glinting off points of rock and giving the impression of teeth, elsewhere casting vicious shadows. Were these jaws to clamp together, they would eat Annette and Balthazar alive.

But not if she ate him first. She'd seen Saber do it to others, and they shared the same sickness, so why not? Nothing mattered anymore, not morals or mercy or love.

Only pain. Only Hell.

Annette scrabbled up rocky inclines and across narrow stone bridges, would catch him, carve him open, and swallow his pieces. She wouldn't cough them up the way Saber had spit Mortimer's entrails into Mr. Calhoun's chair-choked yard. Annette would chew and lick and keep. There would be no body for Balthazar's coffin. Nothing except bones, and she would find a way to grind those down too, indistinguishable from the rest of the wasteland's dust.

Before all that, she would hurt him. For Gloria, Slim, Treasure, and Sylvia. For herself. For Saber.

"For Frank," Annette said, a growl in her throat.

Her echo must have carried; Balthazar's stern voice cut

down the mesa's teeth. "You're aggrieved about your husband."

Annette peered into the gray spaces where descending rays of light brushed with the inner mesa's deep darkness. There was no sign of a preacher's jacket. Where had he gone?

"You think I drove my daughter to your ranch," Balthazar said. "But your troubles predate our coming, do they not? The way you covet that gunslinger. Nurturer of sin, who could say you even loved that man? And yet, you blame me."

Annette groped at sharp ridges and padded up stone ramps. Wherever he'd gone, yes, she blamed him. She half-expected his chest to light up, a beacon to follow, but much better for his light to have run out. No more mandate of Heaven for Balthazar Wilcox, only the desolation where he'd brought her. Hell would fuel her now that Heaven had abandoned him. Misery thrived in this wasteland.

She would start by tearing out his tongue.

"Death was no punishment upon Frank Klein." Balthazar's voice bounded below, and Annette almost turned around to dash down a soft slope. No, only another echo. This place couldn't stop echoing, the way Balthazar wouldn't quit talking. "I couldn't have foreseen my daughter's anguish."

"Couldn't?" Annette almost bit her tongue, turning long behind her lips.

"She would prefer to make herself unworthy, thrashing the way a dreamer might, but there is no awakening until the Lord is born. She is forever the new mother of God." Boots clacked against the stone above. "There is no higher calling. Why would she ever anguish?"

"She didn't have a choice!" Annette shouted. Plain as day, couldn't he see that? He would see less when she tore out his eyeballs.

"The choice was set in precedence by Mary of Nazareth."

"And her choice?"

"The archangel Gabriel spoke to her." There was a rumble in Balthazar's voice as if restraining a sermon's rockslide. "She affirmed."

Annette gritted her teeth. "The hell was she supposed to say?"

"Certainly, what could she say?" Balthazar asked. "How should one oppose God?"

The problem floated outside him, too far to grasp. He could never fathom the difference between his choice of loyalty and the terror a teenage girl had to feel against saying *No*, be that to God, an angel, or a man made in God's likeness. Against that divine immensity, young Mary must have felt like a speck.

Yet despite facing that same power, Saber had resisted. And Balthazar had punished her with the mark.

"There are greater callings than choice," he said. "Had Mary of Nazareth been given a choice, and she declined to mother our Lord, what then? What of the world?"

"What of it?" Annette snapped.

She clambered up a rippling bluff and crossed another stone bridge. She might find Balthazar on either side of the dividing mesa, but bridges zigzagged as far as the light breached inside. She could slip across if she had to. He wouldn't escape.

His voice boomed distantly. "A father knows best, be he earthly or heavenly. God made His choice for mankind, and I made mine for my daughter." Stony fragments clattered high in the ravine. "You're like her, base and blasphemous and proud. Why can't you accept that miracles once more walk among men? Heaven opens, and you deny it. You despise providence."

Annette darted up another incline, crossed another bridge, scrabbled up grooves in the stone, and spilled over a jutting tooth of rock.

No, she didn't despise providence. She despised this place. And him. Hated him. Closer now, she would feel his clothes rumple in her hands, his skin stretch and tear beneath her nails.

"What would you do in my place? Challenge God?" Balthazar had a weight in his voice, more disappointed than angry, as if he expected Annette should know better. "He is the Almighty, and you're a scorned soul, Annette Ruthie Klein."

Quicker, clumsier, up and up, losing her footing twice and dashing along anyway, in and out of light. She thought of Saber, rising and sinking from a smothering nightmare. Handed a burden she didn't want, seeking a way out, torn from her mind and then torn from her mother. Gone forever, lost to everyone but the unwanted child inside.

Annette would slip too, first from a loose natural handhold, and then into the always nightmare, a prize for Frank's ghost. He would drown her again and again in his split-open chest.

Only her fury kept her going. Hellfire would persevere.

Her muscles were sore when she came to the merging of rock teeth, fused into the base of a stone staircase. The steps snaked back and forth along the mesa walls, splitting and reconverging in arcing stone bridges.

Annette clambered up on all fours. She didn't care if her dress shredded away, or if she looked more animal than human. She felt like a beast anyway, chasing her prey up these steps toward the mesa's plateau and leaving nowhere to run. She imagined Big Pete following these steps, smelling her rage in the air, liking it, a tired old bull rejuvenated into a territorial tyrant, his horns destined to plunge through Balthazar's gut and leak his innards. He could go on bleeding from Hell to Slim's Respite and back wherever he'd come from.

"Come," Annette said, half-whispering, half-wheezing. "Don't make me do it alone." One palm scraped over the next step, and the other palm slapped at empty air.

She had reached the top of the steps, but not the top of the mesa. Its ridge formed a horseshoe shape around the ravine. A shelf jutted between the top step and the plateau, where someone seated on the edge could gaze into the ravine's rows of teeth and watch a desperate creature scurry up slopes and steps to reach her prey.

Balthazar's legs dangled over, as whole as he had been when he first appeared to Annette outside the ranch. The ravine didn't seem to interest him now that Annette had reached this height. He stared instead through the crevice and toward the outside, where the white plain stretched to infinity.

"I love this view," he said.

Annette's breath sagged in and out. She looked to see where he was watching and found something besides the flat fields and distant stone.

A fissure climbed in the air like a harsh crack through glass. Pale blue light slithered through in shimmering waves, rocking back and forth with a familiar calm. The longer Annette stared, the more its rhythm soothed her sore muscles, like she knew this sight deep in her blood.

But she didn't want to be calm. She wanted prey. Her eyes tore from the glowing fissure and fixed on Balthazar. He was no miracle here, only a man of flesh and bone. Fragile. Breakable.

"Beautiful, isn't it?" he asked. There was no fear in him, clueless to predators.

He offered her a half-smile and then nodded to the blue fissure. Despite its narrow breadth, its inside stretched deeper than the ravine, inviting the weary to fall inside. It promised to catch them.

"What am I looking at?" Annette asked.

Balthazar took a slow breath. His face eased over his shoulder, and peace filled his eyes. "It is the world."

Annette trailed the ravine's edge until she had almost reached him. Her gaze stuck to the air's fissure. Every coil in the light reflected faint glimpses of brilliance and depth, its world turning and yet unchanging. She wondered if this was the color of the ocean. She had never seen a blue so bright.

CRUEL ANGELS PAST SUNDOWN

"They let the damned watch the world from here?" she asked.

"Here," Balthazar said. Not a question. Yet another echo.

"Hell," Annette said.

Balthazar's smile crept across his face, and he chuckled. "Is that where you think we are?" He stretched to his feet with a tired groan. "Come with me, child of God, and I'll show you the truth." He started up a short incline of stone steps cut into the ridge. They led from the overlook shelf to the mesa's plateau. "Come and see."

The not-sun turned harsher now, brighter, watching Annette the way she had watched the window to the world. She paused in following, her every movement awkward. The sky brightened the higher she climbed until she could hardly see Balthazar ahead. His black preacher clothes melted into light, the same as the dust storm had swallowed him within the stables. Was he leading her back to Low's Bend? She couldn't go, not without Gloria, her horse, and Big Pete, too.

A white glare burned across the mesa. Annette had to narrow her eyes, and yet the light wouldn't crystalize into solid shapes. She could only make out Balthazar's face, the placid line of his mouth, and a dark smile standing out in the radiance, part of another face she'd been desperate to find.

Gloria.

NINETEEN:
THE HEAVENLY PLATEAU

GLORIA'S HAT WAS GONE. So were her duster, pants, pistol, everything Annette had come to know as her lover's usual traveling gear.

A glittering white robe coated Gloria in resplendent light. She sat in a pearlescent ornate seat, fancier than any Annette had ever seen. A lengthy white table curled around her, stuffed with succulent roasts, fluffy loaves of dark bread, sweets seasoned or coated in creams, and colorful fruit bowls carrying juicy berries that Annette didn't recognize. No longer wearing his saddle and bridle, Salt rested on bent legs behind Gloria's seat, drinking from the shimmering pool of a brilliant fountain of crystalline cups, each level spilling the clearest water. Its edges curved along the mesa's marble top.

Annette wanted to shout for Gloria one more time, run to her, but the water called first. She fell to her knees and scooped messy handfuls through her cracked lips, over her dry tongue, and across her face and neck. She must have swallowed as much as Salt before she wrenched back, gasping. The fire inside sputtered, but it couldn't be killed with water.

A shadow broke the pool's glimmer, and Annette turned to a towering figure.

Balthazar was smiling again. "Drink deep," he said. "There is no want in this place."

Annette couldn't fuss with him right now. She looked at the table and the special woman seated there. "What happened to you?" she asked. "I woke up, and you were gone."

"They found me in the night," Gloria said. She chuckled, and her voice curled and reclined like a lazy cat in a favorite ray of sunshine. "When we slept, I should say. The night never comes here."

Above and behind her seat, vast ivory pillars climbed and curved into a sleek archway. Two marble statues of achingly beautiful men crouched to either side of the top, and small wings flowed from their chiseled shoulder blades. The air hung thick between them as if something else should have been built there, but Annette only saw beyond the archway to the not-sun in the sky. This high up, she could make it out more clearly—not a solid spinning halo, but a light formed of winding pieces.

Countless angels, flying round and round. She couldn't tell from here if they resembled these statues, but there was no denying their cold-light presence.

"You see them," Balthazar said, pacing behind her. "They would've escorted you themselves if not for your mark, but you came your own way." He paused to one side and swept an arm toward the pool and feast. "Welcome home, Annette Ruthie Klein. Our true home. Jesus Christ is in Heaven, and so are you."

Annette glanced back to the mesa's ravine, its ridges, and beyond to the open wasteland with its dry-scaled earth and desolate formations. Nothing to drink, nothing to eat, no time, no nightfall, no wind, no birds. Vast pointless emptiness.

"This ain't Heaven," she said, but she wasn't sure. "The desert—"

"We were wrong," Gloria said. "We see what we expect, Butterfly, as we saw in the mesa shadows. Heaven's a strange place that way."

The pool bubbled and frothed where it fed from the

fountain, but its rim never seemed at risk of overflowing. Annette followed its edge to the table, Gloria's seat, and took her hand. She felt as real as she had in another mesa's shadow, in Low's Bend. Real as the first time they'd touched.

"It's no dream," Gloria said, petting Annette's hand. "And there's no need to hide behind excuses anymore, no Frank to give permission. Come, sit on my lap. We can be happy together."

Her face was earnest, her dark eyes twinkling with a reflection of the sky's angelic halo. Annette wanted to kiss her, even with Balthazar standing across the pool, but her body still twitched with fire.

She reached for the table, plucked a grape loose from its vine, and pinched it between her fingertips until its juices dripped. Her tongue, small again, ran along one finger and tasted the sweetness, and then her lips found Gloria's. Yes, it could be Heaven. Yes, it could be good.

A wooden groan creaked across Annette's ears, and she jerked back.

"Did you hear that?" she asked.

Gloria shook her head and smiled, but her eyes flickered to a blue hue across the table.

The fissure lingered against the mesa. Within its world, Annette made out oceans and mountains, thick green forests as she had never imagined, and vast stretches of ice so bright they hurt her eyes. She found a familiar prairie.

The view swept over Low's Bend, a small town turned quiet after one hellish night. There was the house where the Calhoun family lived, and Slim's Respite. Beyond it lay an empty patch where Balthazar's exit had torn the stables from one world into another.

Slim stood in the saloon doorway, a thin silhouette against gray light. Sylvia stood behind him, neither any more injured than Annette had last seen. They were taking down the storm shutters. The view passed the town too quickly for Annette to call out to them. Would they want to hear her after she'd brought a nightmare to Low's Bend? She had to hope so, had to believe a life awaited her, if she could only reach out for it. She had enough cause for vengeance without losing anyone else.

Prairie again filled the fissure, and another figure appeared, but it wasn't anyone else Annette wanted to find tonight.

Instead, she found Saber. Still marked pale, bony, and pregnant, she seemed caught in the wilderness by a billowing fit of soil. The town's dust storm had passed by; this had to be another. Annette felt like she had been wandering this desert for days.

"When she first left me, I followed," Balthazar said, peering up into the blue fissure. "The mark which protected her from herself also stopped me from confining her to home, but I could lessen the wounds she would inflict. Keep the mark from spreading. If I could stop it in her mother, I could stop it in anyone."

The fissure rippled as if it, too, meant to follow Saber. She was lost, drowning in her own red nightmare. No one could help her; no one could harm her.

And yet she was hurting in a way no one understood. The angels had given no real choice, and her father had taken away everything else that mattered—thoughts, future, mother, even her name, unuttered and so lost. Saber's every path had closed. She would have to wait for the child to slide out, and even then, there was no promise the mark would slide away with the afterbirth. Would she again have choices then, or had God decided her part from the beginning?

And now Annette bore the mark, too. What was the end of her road, and had God decided it at the dawn of creation?

"I was given the task to deliver the baby," Balthazar said with a tired sigh. "I was to care for the Lord. An old plan, no longer doable. My body is ravaged; my soul joins the watchers now. Cut off from my daughter's life, and life itself, I can only pray she spreads the mark to no one else in the short time left before the birth." He looked to Annette, and his eyes glittered. "But you could still have a purpose in the world."

Annette started to ask what he meant and then snapped her jaw shut. If she let him into her thoughts, he would take the reins. She would become like Saber in every way.

Balthazar pointed to the fissure. "Return to the world and ensure the Lord is safekept. My daughter is in no fit condition to care for Him, and should He die in the wilderness, we'll have to start all over again. You don't want that. The mark hasn't infected you as deeply as my daughter, not yet."

Annette flexed a hand in front of her face. Her skin seemed paler in the light of the circling angels.

"You bring that baby to good people who will care for Him, and we'll draw you back here," Balthazar said, and he chinned at the table. "And she'll be waiting for you."

"What the hell do you know about us?" Annette snapped. "What went on with me and Frank and others, with me and her, it's more a mess than you could know."

"She told it straightforward. Set your yattering aside, and perhaps try listening to her for a change." Balthazar fitted his hat tighter. "She knows what she wants."

Gloria's gentle hand awaited Annette's. She could have her peace here, and softness, and everything she deserved. Annette could sit with her, and let Heaven take over. Accept that loving hand. Let Frank slide into some forgotten abyss.

"Take me," Gloria said, beaming.

"I would," Annette said, but her hands lingered at her sides.

Why so contrarian? Why not seize this moment? Saber meant nothing; she'd dragged her claws through Annette's life with zero concern for consequences. If destiny intended a sweet eternity with Gloria, there was no reason to fight it. No more secrets, no more keeping them.

CRUEL ANGELS PAST SUNDOWN

The angels swirled above. They might not have had eyes, for all Annette knew, but she felt them watching, as certain as she'd seen that mysterious eye above Low's Bend. Her answer mattered like Saber's never had.

What had Balthazar said? *There are greater callings than choice*. And now this sudden change of heavenly heart.

"Ain't no one can harm me, same as Saber, that right?" Annette asked.

"Because of the mark," Balthazar said.

"The same reason the angels didn't take me. Because of my mark." Annette flexed one hand into a claw and let her fingers stiffen. "Doesn't that mean them taking me would be harm?"

A ripple ran up the mesa's statues, their marble thinning.

"What would you have then?" Balthazar asked. "Child, this is paradise. You'll find nothing sweeter in all of existence. In return, the Lord asks the small favor of bringing Him into the world from my daughter's womb and then carrying Him to where He'll be raised. A brief time safekeeping the new Christ, and then you can have everything you desire. Few souls in all eternity have enjoyed such swift entry into Heaven."

"This ain't Heaven if it's a place of harm," Annette said.

She peered into Gloria's eyes, searching, seeking. Beneath the shine of this illusion, there was the woman who'd taken a piece of Annette's heart and held it, even at the worst times, the hated times. There had to be some of her left inside.

Annette cupped her hands around to Gloria's cheeks. "Be with me."

Gloria's smile was sugar and empty air. "I'm here, Butterfly."

"No, Gloria. We ain't together, and this ain't you. I'm sorry about Frank. I don't know what to do with this heart, it works the way it works, but I loved him, *and* I love you,

147

and I understand if there's no way that's enough." Annette leaned close. "But I need you to wake up. Sometimes there are miles between two people, even when they're standing right beside each other, but I'm reaching out like you've reached for me."

Gloria's smile trembled. Somewhere in the dark of her eyes, the truth lunged to the surface—she had been given no choice. Hauled up here, possessions and body, but without Annette.

Because to come here was a kind of harm.

Saber had known. She'd tried everything she could think of to change her fate. Heavenly power, devils below, her mother, anything to escape the yoke of destiny, but even sharing the mark couldn't tear away God's demands. The angels spoke, but they didn't ask permission. Not with Gloria, not with Saber. In the scripture, Gabriel never asked Mary what she wanted. He only approached, stated what would happen, and she acknowledged it was so. Was that a choice? Mother of God, a merry crown that did not entitle its wearer to any real say in her fate.

Every thought threw kindling inside Annette's furnace. She flinched to tear across the table and claw Balthazar open once and for all.

Through the crack in the air, Saber groaned. Her throat seemed full of creaky hinges to a long-shut door. She had a furnace inside her, too. Beneath the red nightmare, she might still be trying to shut it.

But these doors didn't belong shut. The fury needed to run free. There should never have been a door, no quelling this rage. If every woman could stay angry every moment of her life, and live a hundred lifetimes, she would burn a small hill against the vast mountains of wrath the world deserved.

Annette slipped her hands from Gloria's face and tossed the table aside. Bowls of fruit and platters of bread and meat spilled across the marble and splashed into the pool. Salt lowered his ears as Annette began ranting.

"You like sermons so goddamn much, Balthazar? Tell us one about false idols! What's Heaven do when people don't want it? What's any fire and brimstone when we're burning inside already? Give us a sermon, you piece of preaching shit. I want to know what's the worth in any of this!"

The angel statues blinked into thin air. The archway between them crumbled in a dissipating cloud and rained white dust across the mesa. Fallen food shriveled and melted away, the roast and baked goods and fruit of the earth breaking down into mounds of mud and stone.

Balthazar remained standing, too stubborn to fade into illusion, but he no longer smiled. "Come now, child," he said. "Why couldn't you leave well enough alone and have some faith?"

His eyes fixed first on the halo of angels—they spun closer now, a flock of lantern birds chasing each other—and then on the pool, where a presence grew humid and girthsome.

The air peeled back its lid from the hazy floating shape of a monstrous eye. It had watched Annette from above Low's Bend. It watched her now. An invisible quill scribbled golden letters through the air around its white curve, and a beautiful voice spoke each word as the full visage took shape.

Behold The Archangel.
Gabriel.
Be Not Afraid.

The command quaked through Annette's body, compelling her, but she could only somewhat obey. It was easy to behold the archangel Gabriel as he took full form above the pool; he was too grandiose to do otherwise.

But she couldn't obey the rest of his command. Heart jittering, eyes wide, blood turned cold—she beheld, and she was afraid.

TWENTY:
THE HOST

WHITE FEATHERY WINGS spread from the sides of the slick and inescapable eyeball. They never touched the white orb itself, only swept up and down as if holding it aloft by sheer will. Silver rings bound the eye flesh, and their edges glimmered golden light each time the eyelid swept in a thick-lashed blink. The surrounding golden script twisted and reshaped, in some moments as words in languages and symbols Annette didn't know, at other moments becoming lance-like triangles and complex stars, each catching the sky's glow as if forming constellations.

Nightmare creatures coiled above in a buzzard flock's circle. The flying angels bore lion heads, wheels with faces, and macabre reflections of bone and tooth as if God had been playing practice when forming the Host before trying out these basic principles of life in mortal flesh. There were more angels in Heaven than stars in the cosmos, each too horrible to accept as holy.

And there was no sky—only the Host of distant angels forming every glowing inch.

"It can't be," Annette said. She gazed into Gabriel's eye, where another Annette lived in his pupil's black reflection. "This ain't Heaven."

The golden script swirled around Gabriel. Whatever pen wrote these letters into the air pierced Annette, too, with the archangel's lovely speech.

CRUEL ANGELS PAST SUNDOWN

Behold The Heaven.
The World's Womb.
God's Kingdom Is Whole.

The desolation nagged at Annette's eyes; it demanded she look. "If this is Heaven, where'd you put all the people?"

"You and your questions," Balthazar said. "Heaven keeps wide plains and few residents."

"BEAST. OF. ALL. FAILING." The angel-choked sky burned alight, filling the air with the same tangled mess of voices as had possessed Balthazar's throat in Slim's Respite. "YOU. WILL. BE. SMALL."

Spokes of light cracked down from the halo and slammed Balthazar to his knees. His head dipped over his chest, both arms drooped at his sides, back bending, teeth grinding. He knelt to Gabriel, but the archangel fixed on Annette.

Angelic speech sank into her bones, writing their graceful intent in her marrow.

The Mother Of God Knows Not Herself.
Nameless Bearer To The Mark Of Cain.
Wanderer To The Land Of Nod.
By Her Suffering, Comes The Lord.
By Death, We Bring The Almighty.

Annette's knees wobbled. She was meant to kneel like Balthazar and find some solace in obedient piety. What happened to Saber would only partly happen to her. She could join Gloria still if she buckled and let the angels have their way. Give in, let well enough alone. This was not Annette's house to set right.

"Why do all this?" she asked. "You say it's Heaven, but where's God?"

New letters slithered around Gabriel, but they didn't form concrete words. Annette thought his crystalline voice might rise to shout her down, tell her she was too lowly a creature to question angels, let alone God. If Balthazar was a small nuisance, she had to be worthless.

The halo of angels thundered. "THE. PRESENCE. LEFT. US."

"The Lord would have to leave Heaven to be born," Annette said. "This ain't your first rodeo. You've forced one such conception way back already."

Gabriel's iris thinned around his swelling pupil.

The Presence Left Before.
But Soon, A Return.

Balthazar lifted his head beneath the oppressive light and opened his mouth to sing:

O then bespoke our Savior, all in His mother's womb:
'Bow down, good cherry tree, to my mother's hand.'

The circling halo fumed, and this time the entire sky of angels quaked. "YOU. WILL. BE. SILENT."

Golden letters formed around Gabriel again. Annette shut her eyes not to see them, but their meaning stroked her ears anyway.

Your Purpose Has Ended.
In Failure.
God Be With You.

The great eye swelled. The center blackness widened, becoming more a mouth than a pupil. Balthazar gritted his teeth as Gabriel touched his arm. Cold air rushed across the pool as if Balthazar had thrown open the window of a charging train car. The pupil drew him in, first by hand, and then to his shoulders, and then the rest.

He gaped wide-eyed and desperate at Annette. Tears rushed down his cheeks. She flinched to help but stopped herself. Why the urge to save him after everything he'd done? He deserved whatever terrible end the archangel could give.

He sank back into the sticky black pond. His legs vanished into the archangel's eye, and his torso. His head vanished inch by inch until his tear-stained face sucked in one last gulp of air.

He thrust open his mouth in a desperate shout. "Jesus Christ! Is in Heaven!"

CRUEL ANGELS PAST SUNDOWN

Oily darkness swallowed the hairline, temples, and jaw. Balthazar blinked one last time, his eyelids sliding slowly down, open again, and for a moment the blackness of his eyes looked out from Gabriel's cyclopean pupil.

And then he was gone.

Writing flitted around Gabriel's wings, some new command churning in him alongside Balthazar.

"He's wrong, ain't he?" Annette asked.

The writing settled into place. Gabriel's wings drooped, and some of the shine went out of the shapes sliding between his airy golden script.

Jesus Christ Is In Hell.

The fire inside Annette floundered. Gabriel had to mean the world, America, maybe the western territories and their deserts and prairie, where Saber wandered with a baby inside. Annette couldn't be sure, and she didn't know how to ask. The harsh emptiness of this wasteland made her wonder.

Gabriel pivoted above the pool. His eyeball seemed no heavier for carrying Balthazar. Its pupil might have already digested him. Another swirl of golden writing shimmered around loose feathers.

In His Infinite Compassion.
Our Lord Long Ago Descended.
To Wash The Feet Of Sinners.
He Has Abdicated His Throne.
Until He Has Saved Every Soul.

The sky rippled with offended angels. "BEHOLD. AN. IMPOSSIBLE. TASK."

Part of a parable slid into Annette's thoughts. Balthazar would have been proud. "He would leave no lamb lost," she said.

Gabriel shined with a halo of writing.

The Highest Order Of The Host.
Has No Lord To Contemplate.
To Praise.
He Has Relieved The Seraphim.
And Joined The Fallen.

The Host surged with light. "WE. HAVE. NO. PURPOSE."

Annette's skin itched. The radiance infected every inch of her, intent to crush her in holy desperation. She laid a hand across her chest and found her heart racing. Desperation hung thick in the air. Heaven or not, this place was angry. She knew the feeling.

But the angels' despair made no sense. "Who left you?"

Gabriel's pupil flicked back and forth as if he couldn't make sense of her question.

"You want Christ reborn, but where's God?" The halo flared above, and Annette looked to the angel-bloated sky. "You still ain't answered. Don't you know?"

Gabriel spoke again:

The Presence Is Absent.
The Light Descends.

Annette recoiled. There was no authority here. The angels were only children playing with what some heavenly father had left to them. She would do better to interrogate Big Pete if she needed a pointless task.

Was she misunderstanding something about God, or was Gabriel? His one big eye might have seen the presence differently than she did, an ancient life against her relatively young one, and yet she felt older than mountains. The pale mark was aging her to Genesis, to times unknown. Gabriel might have seen much and known little. Annette couldn't guess.

His pupil refocused on her.

The Presence Has Left Us Bereft.
We Have Chosen To Guide Him.

"Guide to what exactly?" Annette asked.

She couldn't guarantee a real answer. The archangel gave some absolute yet confusing gradience in his speech that left too many questions and precious little understanding. *Presence* could mean many things, and she couldn't guess where Christ fit into it. She didn't know how to ask, and Gabriel didn't know how to answer.

CRUEL ANGELS PAST SUNDOWN

He swelled with proud luminance, and the writing formed new and glorious letters as if to look on them was to feel their weight.

A New Incarnation.
Will Change Our Lord.
As Did His First To Love.
He Will Return Anew.
A Wrathful, Pitiless Lord.
Who Will Not Love The Damned.
Who Will Not Abandon Heaven.
The Host Will Rejoice.

Annette's thoughts sank into the red nightmare. Narrow, humid, a pulse running through this imitation of Frank's cut-open chest, the wetness and blood were almost comforting against the cruel wasteland and its harsh cold answers.

She had been asking *why* since the beginning. Why had Saber murdered Frank? Balthazar had cursed her. And why had Balthazar done so? Saber meant to rid herself of divine burden. And why had she ever carried it?

Here flew the reason, and his name was Gabriel. His sweet golden script pierced even the red nightmare and stiffened Annette to full attention.

Child Of God.
Return To The Creation.
Tend The Lord.
We Will Give Balthazar.
Before He Is Consumed.
For Your Wrath.
We Will Give Gloria.
For Your Love.
Cherish Revenge And Paradise Alike.

Everything began sinking, and Annette fought to keep her head up from the red nightmare within.

Gloria sat wide-eyed in her seat. Annette could take her hand and end this pain. Gabriel offered the same as Balthazar, except with vengeance on a preacher to sweeten the deal.

Anything Annette wanted, so long as the angels got their way.

And if they didn't? If Balthazar's concern came true and the new baby God died on the prairie, somewhere east of Low's Bend, maybe halfway to Monteau Station? Nothing would stop the angels from trying again. There would be no punishment for angels.

If their plan didn't work, they would repeat. And repeat. They would keep impregnating people until they got their way. Never any choice. Like Slim had said, getting put up with a child they didn't want? *It could happen to any of us.*

But it shouldn't have happened to anyone. And Frank should have lived. Gloria should have found true peace outside this heavenly nightmare.

Annette glared into Gabriel's eye, and her reflection glared back. "Did you ask Gloria what she wanted?"

Gabriel's feathers twitched. Again, he didn't understand.

"How do you know she wants eternity with me?" Annette asked, a growl in her voice. "How do you know she likes this place? Likes me? She might not love me anymore, but you don't know what that means. She might be sick to death of me. I'm difficult that way. You never asked her. Never respected her choices, her feelings. You don't got the first idea with her. You're nothing but God's bastards, and you don't know a goddamn thing."

Fire surged up Annette's throat. She should shut the door—no, that was a learned reflex, some other Annette-like thought preserved from before this nightmare's beginning.

She knew better now. The furnace door belonged open, its doorway roaring aflame. Every muscle twitched to lash out at Gabriel, pour herself across him, tooth and nail and tongue, to carve angel flesh the way Saber had carved Frank, except she had used a blade and Annette would claw with body and soul.

CRUEL ANGELS PAST SUNDOWN

Gabriel's pupil rippled.

Your Answer.
To The Offer.

"You can't give me Gloria," Annette said. "She's hers, and I'm mine, and if we want to give ourselves to each other, that ain't your business. As for Balthazar, I don't want his blood." She bared her teeth and curled her hands into claws. "I want yours."

TWENTY-ONE:
AGAINST ALL HEAVEN

THE SKY OF ANGELS roared ferocious light, and their circling halo grew more vulture-like. Given the chance, they would tear Annette down and scavenge flesh from her body. It seemed an angel's truest nature.

White radiance poured through Gabriel's wings.

Do You Challenge The Host?

"What's the Host without God?" Annette asked. "God ain't here. What do you call Heaven now?"

All Of Creation Empowers Us.

The Arbiters Of Heaven.

"Heaven." Annette spat into the pool and watched the water ripple. "Where's Frank?"

Frank.

"Frank Klein," Annette snapped. "My husband."

Gabriel sank an inch toward the pool. His twitching eye looked lost as if a hundred Annettes gathered behind her and he didn't know which to face.

Why Presume To Find Him Here?

"Because he was a good man. Put up with a lot of me, like Gloria has, and your new mother of God murdered him in cold blood." Annette inched toward the pool's rim. If she could walk on water, she would charge across and spit in Gabriel's eye. "If this is Heaven, where's Frank?"

The water broke into waves beneath Gabriel. His words lost none of their beautiful resonance as they sharpened to blades.

CRUEL ANGELS PAST SUNDOWN

Meager, Doubtful Creature.
You Question For You Covet.
A Longing To Be The Lord's Mother.
To Heal Your Barren Womb.

The nightmare carried Frank's face into Annette's head. She hadn't known whether he was the reason for there being no children, or if something inside her made them impossible. But Gabriel seemingly had the power to tell.

Annette clawed back from the nightmare to reality. No point letting this angel distract her. The state of her womb changed nothing.

"That's right, he wanted children," she said. "And it would've broken his heart to know I was relieved it never happened. A good man like him sure ain't in Hell. You tell me we've reached Heaven, but I don't believe you because Frank is nowhere to be seen. Where then? Quit stalling and tell me where we really are."

Malformed script encircled Gabriel. The invisible quill scrawled bent triangles and broken stars, but no words.

Annette's face curled into a sneer. Her reflection in the eye sneered back, and she hoped Gabriel felt it. "This here's no Heaven. This here is nothing but a shed out Heaven's back, storing up old tools and supplies God's forgotten how to use because they hardly got purpose anymore. He decided there's no more need for angels, ain't that right?"

A hand snatched Annette's wrist. She reeled around to scratch a face, expecting some new angelic trick.

Her claw froze when she met Gloria's eyes. Her real eyes. She rocked back and forth, a sleeper thrashing against an unending dream.

"Wake up," Annette said through clenched teeth. "Come on, Gloria. Come back to me."

Gloria's head jerked hard to one side with a startled hiss. Her eyes blinked, slow and heavy, and then she turned a firm scowl at Annette. The glittering white robe peeled away, a curtain dropping from her real clothes, dusty and worn, smelling of road and people. The brim of her hat again encircled her head. Her free hand twitched at one side, eager for a pistol's grip. She turned damp eyes to Annette.

"You make it hurt to come back," Gloria said, and her voice was prettier than any angel's.

Annette kissed her, fast and hard and fiery, and then again with softness. There wasn't time for a third before she coughed out, "I'm sorry."

"It was smothering." Gloria stood wobbly from her seat. Unease coated her face in sweat, and she looked like she might be sick. "I saw and heard, but I couldn't move or speak."

The pale sky glowed gold-white. "WE. OFFERED. YOU. PURITY."

Gloria shook the sick look away and straightened her back to face the Host. "What would you know about purity?" she asked. "You are empty echoes, and without your Lord to speak, you've nothing to repeat. You're no one, not pure, not wrong, all a big bunch of nothing. You could leave, but you don't know how. You could live, but you don't understand the point. Never tried. He had to live and die and find a new purpose. Could you echo your Lord that way?"

Annette stared at Gloria. She had said she was no adventurer, nothing like the romantic idea Annette had painted in her head, but some part of Gloria couldn't help glowing with magnificence. Appearing through the saloon doors, her coat whipping behind her. Those soft moments when she let her guard down.

And right now, glaring at a sky made of angels.

"There's no weight to your praise and glory if you don't understand what it means," she went on. "When have you lot ever smelled a newborn baby? Been hungry, or cold, or frightened, or anything at all? When was the last time you stopped chanting holiness and stepped outside Heaven's shadow to help someone? Never. Never in the eternity of God's love."

CRUEL ANGELS PAST SUNDOWN

A sky-splitting scream rocked the mesa. The white wasteland buckled under the cacophony.

Annette took Gloria's arm. "You need to get out of here. Hop onto Salt and go."

Gloria scowled at her. "Get?"

"You got a life to live, remember?" Annette stole a moment for one more quick kiss. "Live it. You deserve all the peace you can get."

"You can't stay here alone," Gloria said.

Annette turned from Gloria's eyes to her own cursed-pale skin. She knew its namesake now, and it didn't scare her. "What can they do to me?" she asked. "God's servants against God's will?"

Gloria grasped Annette's arms and pulled her close. "I shouldn't have thought what we have doesn't mean anything. It does. It's complicated, but it means something."

Annette let herself sink into Gloria's embrace. If they made it out of this wasteland, she would find a way to mend every hurt between them. Not perfect—never perfect—but some way to bridge her feelings before she turned out like Saber and felt nothing at all.

Before that, she would make sure Gloria could go on.

Their embrace broke apart, Gloria's eyes brimming with red tears. Annette wanted to believe her heart had been so full that it poured out her eyes, but that was nonsense. The mark had gained a foothold inside Annette, its sickness taking root deeper through her body. Maybe Gloria meant to cause harm. Maybe that was how love worked.

Annette's lucidity slipped toward heavy darkness again. She turned half-lidded eyes to Gabriel. He would call the Host to crush them now, the way he had Balthazar, flatten them beneath the cold brilliance of angelic determination.

But Gabriel teetered. A quake rocked loose feathers from his wings, and his tremendous lashes quivered like a hundred waving arms. Golden script jittered around him, each word dribbling into the others as if a freshly inked page had been set over a candle. His upper lid seemed to droop across the top of his iris, and an underlid of tar filled the lower rim with black tears.

Why would an angel cry? Did he feel anything but desperation? Annette caught a scent in the air—not copper like she'd smelled from Frank's or Balthazar's blood. A smell trapped somewhere between the white-hot burning when Balthazar had murdered Treasure and a new scent Annette couldn't recognize.

The tar dripped down one swirling silver ring and struck the pool of water, where it spread in a black cloud.

These weren't tears. An angel could bleed.

Saber's familiar croak climbed Annette's throat. "Do. It."

Gabriel's lid slid up again. Each wing spread as he loomed closer, and his script sharpened around him.

You Do Not Command The Host.

Annette's fingers twitched at her sides, eager to grab some phantom pistol, but that was Gloria's business. She had her bare hands. What could disgust a holy angel worse than the filth of God's creation?

"Do it," Annette croaked again. "Hurt me. Do it!"

A tinge of darkness cracked through Gabriel's iris. The mark had reached out for him. Did he see the red nightmare? What else did he see? And if he couldn't hurt Annette, could she hurt him?

Her hands curled into wicked claws, and she launched at the monolithic eye. The flesh might not have the same texture as a humans, and she couldn't be sure angels would feel pain, but she would try to teach Gabriel that mortal experience.

Her nails raked across the underside of his lower lid—nothing. She clawed at the white eye flesh, the iris. She couldn't reach his wings without running to either side, and she wouldn't give him the chance to turn from her and punish Gloria.

"Hurt me, right now, do it!" Annette screamed, and she hoped that Saber could hear through the fissure to the world.

Annette reeled back one arm and plunged a claw into Gabriel's pupil, where her reflection likewise reached for her. Her hand jammed through black flesh.

The world tilted. Her feet left the ground as the inside of the angel's eye changed all directions to down. She was sinking, and Gabriel was a muddy pit, grasping and pulling, bigger inside than out, the way the back wall of the stables had opened to this stark wasteland. His once-beautiful voice rang with an eerie cadence.

Behold The Archangel.
Gabriel.
And Be Afraid.

Annette lost sight of the sky, the plateau, Gloria. Her world clouded until there was nothing to see. She thrashed one arm back as if she could catch the rim of Gabriel's iris, but there was only cold sludge.

Inside the archangel, there spread infinite darkness.

Annette clawed wild in every direction, but fluid slipped through her fingers. Gabriel's innards had no walls, no floor or ceiling, and no complex chambers of organs and tubes. He was only this endless pool.

How to stop this? How to get out before he hurt Gloria?

Annette tried to run, but her legs churned against mud. She couldn't be sure how she even breathed here. Distance didn't matter; there was no end, like dashing in a circle and expecting to get somewhere. She might have been running in place.

"I can't—" Annette started and then gritted her teeth.

A wintery chill sank through her. She couldn't feel her feet anymore. Numbness crept up her legs, thighs, and middle. She flexed and unflexed one hand and then lashed out.

And touched something firm in the dark fluid.

Its words scurried up her fingers. "Why has God forsaken me?" a familiar voice asked. "Beth, I'm sorry."

"Balthazar?"

"God." A pained croak took over Balthazar's voice. "Why?"

That merciful twinge hit Annette's heart. She was pitying him again; she couldn't help it. Had Balthazar met her husband, he wouldn't have understood Frank's strong gentleness, bashful heart, his curiosity, or his love. Balthazar was almost like an angel, hollow except for what was expected of him. What a sad life. And a sad death, too.

Annette reached out. "Balthazar, wait!"

"Why?" he asked again.

Annette's fingers swept after him. Indiscernible lumps slipped through her grasp.

"Why?" His groan wore through angelic insides, and the echo of his question writhed across Annette's bones. "Why?" The world bubbled, and the echo faded. No Balthazar lingered in word or body.

Gabriel had consumed him.

Annette remembered earlier tonight—last night?— lying in Treasure's bed and asking the same question with a thousand implications. Neither tears nor answers would save her now. If she stopped feeling, she would stop existing. This place would slip under her mark to her true skin and beneath, to muscle and bone. It would fill her and consume her, making her no different than the rest of Gabriel's insides. His pupil was a stomach, ready to tear her apart and digest her. Didn't that count as harm? She didn't know the rules inside angels. She was the one who'd lashed out; he'd only let her, and now she was here.

But he must've known she would slip inside him. It was the easiest way to be rid of her.

Cold overtook her skin and soaked her muscles. Scraping, jerking, wriggling—if she couldn't feel, was she really moving, or did she only wish she could?

She raked jagged nails down her wrist. The pinch came in pitiful insect bites. She dug harder, seeking nerves, veins, and vast depths of pain. Anything to stay awake, stay here, keep feeling.

A red crater cracked open through her thoughts—the nightmare. She had already been drowning through the night, ever since Saber came to the ranch house. Not in Gabriel's black pupil, but in the ravages of Frank's death and Saber's curse. Nothing new.

And here he was. Those eyes. That mustache. The judgment and the haunting. She could smell him, not only the coppery stink of blood but *him*, of dirt and animal and the distinct human smell of her husband, Frank Klein. Had Gabriel eaten him, too?

Frank shook his head and flashed a wry warmth like he was about to say something ridiculous to lure out her smile.

What is it? Annette wanted to ask. *What's the joke this time, Frank?*

There were no words. If anything was the joke, it was her. A look, a strange way of speaking, some body language uniquely hers that he would never explain, but it lit up his eyes. How could a man who loved her so much haunt her now, even if every awful thing had been her fault? He would forgive.

Oh. Annette's heart thrummed. She understood now.

Frank was not a vengeful man, and he had never been the kind to hurt, let alone to haunt. So why poison his memory? Did she think that would make missing him any lighter, make happiness with Gloria any easier? Poison would only spread, as vile as a pale mark.

It was wrong to pretend he was a ghost in her head. He would've already forgiven her.

And he deserved better than the death he got. Annette couldn't change that for him, but at the least, he deserved to be remembered right. Not as part of the red nightmare, but as himself. It wasn't his fault she never told him the truth, never got to say sorry about his death or anything else. Never said goodbye.

"Be well, my Frank." That would have to do; the easy part. The hard part would come if she survived, having to try her best at enjoying everything to come for however long she had left to live. Give Gloria the whole heart and everything she deserved. Or let her go, to find her peace and better future. Annette could do that much, at least.

And instead of blaming herself anymore, better to focus on who was really to blame. Who had started it.

She could not let these bastards win.

Fire billowed up Annette's throat, hot and angry and human. The furnace door warped against the heat, cracked down the middle, and began to burn.

Frank had not been a vengeful man, but she was another kind of woman altogether. Maybe he'd loved that secret part of her before she'd known it was there. She hoped so.

"You did this," Annette said. "You damn angels, and your nothing purpose. All that pain, for what? Frank's dead, and that's the end. He's dead, and it's your fucking fault."

She thrashed against the muddy darkness. It swelled and swam around her limbs, but she wouldn't stop clawing, kicking, and biting.

"You couldn't handle being tossed aside, and you made us do your dirty work, but you didn't give her a choice. You didn't give any of us a choice!"

She lunged headfirst and open-mouthed against the dark and chewed at the thick black fluid. It ran cold down her throat, but it fed her fire like oil, and she bit again. And again.

Gabriel didn't understand people. He thought only he could consume others and carry on for eternity, but Annette had a stomach too. She tore faster, swallowed, stoked her furnace, and made the archangel one with her insides. Saber had known what to do all along when she began eating men's flesh.

Annette's tongue thickened down her mouth until it

lolled out, a snake coiling around the darkness. It dragged pieces screaming between her teeth, down her throat. Gabriel's insides weakened and trembled. He must've never known fire like this before.

Light peeked through the darkness—a destination.

Annette fought harder, digging, lapping, devouring. The fluid of Gabriel's eye swelled thicker than any drink, but she swallowed and kept swallowing, throat throbbing. She didn't stop digging and eating until the light took her, and she spilled in a freefall onto the marble plateau.

Firm hands held her—Gloria.

"Annette?" she asked. "Give us a word, love."

Talking would hurt, and there was nothing to say. Annette clambered up Gloria's arms to her feet and turned the fountain, the pool, and the archangel.

Gabriel faltered toward the water's surface. His pupil spouted like a burst oil vein and spilled blackness into the pool. His monstrous eye was a cored apple, broken on the inside and rotted through the skin. Silver rings clanked against marble and splashed into the pool below. Golden script melted from his halo and rained across the plateau, each syllable a cacophony of brass gongs. The pool drank him in, and its water broke apart his body as if dissolving a clump of earth. Only his wings remained floating in a dazzle of splayed feathers.

"Butterfly," Gloria said, reaching out. "Is it you? You're alright?"

The questions were too complicated. Was Annette alright? She didn't know. She stared into the pool, waiting for Gabriel to rise, but if there was some core to him, she had eaten it. Made it part of her. He would rise again as fuel for her violence and fury, but not as God's servant again.

A glittering reflection caught in the pool's surface, and she turned skyward. Black angel blood soaked through her teeth and down her neck and chest.

Swirling radiance descended, the Host spiraling

against the mesa's plateau. "YOU. HAVE. DEFILED. HIM." The sky became chipped glass, and angels rained across the wasteland.

Annette wanted to tell them Gabriel had brought defilement first, to show them a raw wound in eternity, festering and unclean and rotting every good thing they touched.

But speaking would show them nothing. They needed to know tooth and claw.

Their golden-white light filled the plateau. Annette curled her claws and rushed into them.

There was no panic this time. She wasn't a rancher, or a widow, or a lover anymore. There was nothing to her in this moment except the frantic need to carve through the holy Host.

They weren't anywhere near as large as Gabriel. When she plunged her hands into their faces, she didn't sink inside. She found what she wanted with each fistful of angel flesh, the way Saber had pulled their influence from Balthazar's head. Black lumps, oozing and cold.

Annette finished where Saber couldn't—she stuffed angelic flesh into her mouth by the handful. One from a lion-headed abomination. Another from the face upon a turning wheel. Every twisted creature fell to her slashing and her licking and her swallowing. Their numbers were endless, with more angels in Heaven than stars in the sky, far beyond her power to count.

But she was nothing like they had ever faced before. God's declaration lived in her skin, and the door inside her piled in ashes, her fire raging free through the red nightmare, as bottomless as her fury. Their wars had always pitted angel against angel.

They didn't know the ferocious terror of humanity. She would eat every angel, even if the feast took all eternity.

The Host soon broke into desperate swarms and began to scatter. Annette grasped at fleeing angels and clawed them open, devouring their insides.

CRUEL ANGELS PAST SUNDOWN

But they were a broken body, no longer speaking in their strange, conjoined speech. Now they screeched the odd music of a panicked animal unused to fear. They flew in all directions, out across the wasteland, to the sky, and hazy night-like darkness seeped where their numbers thinned into the distance. The wasteland would soon become a dark place, night having found it at last.

Fire flitted in Annette's throat. It had never burned so harshly before, and there was a sort of peace in the sated flames.

She lowered her hands to hips and stood heaving, drenched head to toe in angelic blood. Through the dark murk, she watched the remaining Host spread to the horizon. They were too distant to look like wheels and bones and monsters anymore, reduced to dwindling faraway lights, almost shooting stars. No authority, no choir of any kind. They would hesitate before thinking up hollow-headed plans again.

The wasteland grew quiet and windless as the sky dipped into gloom. Gloria scooped water from the pool and wiped Annette's face. Gabriel had tainted the fountain, and this water could only clean so much, but Annette let caring hands do their best. There would be worse work ahead.

She looked beyond Gloria, to a shimmering fissure in the air. Oceans sang a sweet rhythm, and between them, a vast land offered familiar comforts.

TWENTY-TWO:
THE BEGINNING AND THE END

ANOTHER ROLLING DUST storm ebbed from the world, and the lingering soft wind brushed Annette's skin as she stepped onto the prairie. She couldn't remember ever having missed the breeze before following Balthazar into that other world. Now she hoped the air would never hold still again.

Crows cawed in the distance. She couldn't see them, but their cries let her know they were here, that this was a place of animals, and sometimes they died and others fed on them, and life went round and round in ways no angel could comprehend.

Gloria stepped with her, and the wind sharpened a little so that she had to put a hand on her hat to keep it still. Her smile said she didn't mind. She had missed the wind, too, and the turning of the sky, the sun changing places, time carrying from dawn toward dusk.

The world held all these little miracles beyond Heaven's comprehension.

Hooves patted the dirt behind Annette and Gloria. Annette had traveled down the ravine to lead Big Pete toward the plateau and the way back to the world. Salt followed in turn. She didn't know what would become of the few remaining horses, but she hoped they would find some way through, too. There had to be other exits. She could only help the big bull she and Frank had cared for climb a slow, dangerous road to the great mesa's top, where she and Gloria led their animals to the prairie and roads. To Saber.

No, not Saber—Beth. Beth Wilcox.

If she heard them, she paid no mind, staggering on as she walked alone. They followed her past a lazy river, where Gloria filled her waterskins and let the animals drink.

Annette kept following without pause. She meant to keep that pale naked form in sight. In the bright light of morning, she noticed soiled patches patterning Beth's body, the residue she wore from the elements. She wouldn't be harmed, but she seemed too weary to clean herself now.

They walked until mid-afternoon. The sun had reached the middle of the western sky when Beth at last crumpled. First to her knees, then flat on her back, and her saber clanged against a flat stone.

Gloria started forward and then stumbled, her head rocking side to side. She couldn't help with this part. Bad enough that her eyes bled if she came too close to Annette, but Beth was worse. There was no point right now in trying to understand what the future might look like. There was only this moment, and Beth, and the quake in her womb.

The baby was coming.

Annette crept closer, one eye watching that cavalry saber. Beth pressed her forearms to the earth and made no move to lift it. The pain had found her for the first time since Balthazar and the angels put the mark of Cain across her body. If Annette had doubted Gabriel's words and plans, the agony breaching even this divine curse was proof of some greater force coming than any ordinary birth.

Yet still a child, and every trial that entailed. Annette circled Beth, knelt between her legs, and whispered encouragement she probably couldn't hear, urged her to breathe, and maybe a prayer slipped in, too. The sun slid deeper behind the mountains, and Beth's body jittered in the purpling dusk.

Annette had heard a sermon once detailing the birth of Jesus from Joseph's point of view. The minister recounted that the sky had filled with angels and trumpets, that stars had exploded across the desert night, and soon the entire cosmic order buckled in on itself to watch the infant Lord enter the world.

Joseph had been small then, a mortal man shaken with terror and awe. But he'd had the free time to gaze at the sky while his wife's son was born.

If any such ceremony spilled over the prairie this evening, Annette didn't notice. She had her hands full with the splashing blood and shit and clumps of flesh, the dirty work of birth those ancient holy men never wrote about in the scripture. She wondered briefly what those pages might tell had Mary of Nazareth written of her son's birth herself, but the thought flitted away when a miracle slid into Annette's arms.

There was a round head, covered in wet birth. Ten fingers, ten toes, a tight curling face. Annette cleaned around the eyes, nose, and mouth, and then pried Beth's saber from her fingers to cut the navel cord from mother and child. Afterbirth slid behind and lay in the earth. Annette then cut away the lower edges of her dress and swaddled the baby in bloodstained blue fabric. He would be secure for now.

Beth panted through her open mouth and gazed at the bruise-colored sky. She likely swam the red nightmare, and Annette couldn't help her there. She would have to resurface on her own, and even then, would she know her child's face? Gabriel had made recognition sound unlikely. In time, Annette would be the same, a creature made nearly mindless by the mark.

But what did he know? Angels never brought life into this world, and miracles to them were no brighter than fireflies.

Gloria chanced getting near long enough to drape her duster over Beth's nakedness. Annette rocked the baby back and forth, taking a moment to breathe in the miracle and soak in the warmth.

One echo had followed her from the wasteland. Not of memory, but the dream of a good man. Frank had so badly wanted to see her holding a messy little newborn like this one in her arms. He would have watched, almost afraid to touch, but then he would've mustered the bravery to cradle their child. Any little baby would have been soothed in his firm yet gentle arms, knowing before any words or thoughts that he was safe. He would give the child a strong home and teach that sometimes hearts found mending better in a little friendliness than in a sermon.

Nothing could mend Annette's splintered heart. No child would be safe with her for long. Red dots were already forming in this one's eyes, and she skittered back from Beth.

"Do you want to?" she asked, arms outstretched to Gloria, almost insistent.

Gloria patted Salt's neck and strode close to take the baby. Red tears brimmed along her eyes at Annette's nearness, but she ignored them and gazed down at an innocent face, delicate beyond imagining. He had that raw special smell like any newborn.

But this was not just any newborn.

"Should we give a name before we—" Gloria pursed her lips and let her question float away in the wind.

"Names sometimes keep going after we're gone." Annette ran her fingers over the baby's head. "He doesn't want this night remembered. Not like last time."

She couldn't say how she knew. The thought bled into her and pooled deeper than the red nightmare. Divine desire had taken Frank's place behind her eyes.

She drew the baby from Gloria's arms, held the bundle close to smell again, and imagined Frank's puzzlement over why she would do such a thing. She wouldn't have explained, only held the baby up to his nose, and then he would have understood. He'd been good at understanding.

Maybe, if she had given him the chance, he would have accepted how she hadn't wanted to grow one of her own in her womb.

He might even have accepted why she had to carry this baby toward a twisted line of dry brush, far from Gloria, Beth, and the animals, and lay the bundle on the soft earth of the prairie.

He fussed tiny fists against the ragged dress. Annette caressed that tiny head, kissed that soft brow, and then slinked back to Gloria. Every muscle in her wanted to cradle the baby again, the fire in her demanding not fury but something else.

She retreated until she could hardly make out a bundle of stained blue against the prairie's rough flora. This was how it had to be.

"How long?" Gloria asked.

"Not long," Annette said, her voice drained. "He would have to want to stay for the end to take long."

The first hour slid past, and the last light of dusk seeped out of the sky. Night descended with an unseasonable chill as if a sudden winter had answered the call of some unearthly force. Gloria built a scant campfire of dry brush and thin twigs, and she shared the remaining jerky from Salt's pack. Annette wanted to feed Beth, but she didn't know how. There were no people here to eat, and this new mother of God hadn't moved since the birth except for panting out quick breaths.

They had nothing to feed the baby, either, but that mattered less. They ate, and then they tried to talk about normal things, like road travel and sights and the weather.

When those topics died in their smallness, Annette and Gloria watched the fire twist and dance. There was some distance between them at first, but little by little, Gloria scooched nearer, bringing her warmth against the cool night. She flashed Annette a tender look and raised one hand, maybe to take Annette's chin, look in her eyes, and share a gentle kiss.

CRUEL ANGELS PAST SUNDOWN

Annette excused herself to fetch more water. She didn't want to watch Gloria cry red tears. Annette couldn't be Beth, bringing symptoms of the mark to the people she loved. Especially not after everything Gloria had endured, and not after what they'd said to each other in that wasteland.

"Annette," Gloria said upon Annette's return. She grew rigid for a moment and then shook herself as if sensing a brisk wind. "Never mind. I lost what I meant to say. Forget it, Butterfly."

Annette looked to Gloria's hands, her arms, her cheek, wishing to kiss every part of her. But Gloria had said not to break her heart, and Annette couldn't be sure to keep a promise like that anymore. Something important might have slipped away in whatever Gloria had meant and forgotten to say.

Or maybe Annette was the trouble. She had accepted Frank as an understanding man after he was already gone. Would she make the same mistake now, or would she accept Gloria as an understanding woman?

She scratched at her arms as if her nails could carve away the mark of Cain, and then she sat on the far side of the flames. This was a safer place to watch Gloria. To exist together.

They listened to the campfire crackle against the harmony of insect-song and distant coyote howls. Even if they weren't sure what to say anymore, something was always loud and alive in the prairie night.

And dying, too.

The wind howled when it happened, rustling brush and campfire. The earth seemed to tilt between Annette and Gloria as if grains of soil were running through an open hole in the world.

And then the wind stilled. No light cracked across the darkness, and no stars flared or burst. This was not the cosmic buckling Joseph had witnessed. Whatever had changed came quick and then was gone. Annette couldn't be certain what came next, the message unclear inside her, but she guessed there had been no ascension. Gabriel was dead, and this was the end.

Gloria ran her sleeve beneath each eye, soaking tears and blood. "Where we were," she said. "Do you think it really was Heaven once?" Her stained cheeks glimmered in the firelight. She wasn't looking at Annette. "I wonder what it's like when it's the way it should be. If there is such a notion as *should*."

Annette had no answers.

Perhaps the presence now gone from the world did not know either. He might have only been a shepherd after all, confused some days about the weather, or the movements of the flock, and yet trying, like everyone in the world was trying.

Annette saw it in her dreams that night, a quiet, peaceful light, the first to ever descend into an eternal stretch of darkness and dust where the damned once scurried, sightless, thoughtless, hopeless. The presence had come, and the angels had drawn it away from these poor souls.

Now they wandered again toward the renewed light, across sins and centuries.

If this beacon meant to bring them all into a holy embrace, there might be those who would resist, and that was fine. He would wait, for even without another mortal incarnation, the presence might learn something new. Why create a world of such people with such wills and imaginations if not to break bread with them, to change and grow as they did?

Why persist across eternity if not to see the value in every mortal creature?

The night slid by. A harsh paranoia made Annette worry the sun wouldn't rise in the morning, that she had thrown it from the world with the child's death, but a red dawn climbed in the east as it always had, as if winking away an absent nightmare.

CRUEL ANGELS PAST SUNDOWN

She clambered up from the smoking remains of the campfire, where Gloria slept fitfully. Part of her wanted to curl at Gloria's side. Another better part of her knew, for all their complications and the something between them, the mark might be the final wedge that drove them apart. She wouldn't watch Gloria's eyes bleed again.

A few yards away, Beth slept too, calmer somehow. She looked different, hued almost crimson in the light of sunrise. Almost as peaceful as Gloria.

Annette left them to search the dry brush. There was one last task before this was over, when she could worry over what lay ahead for herself and Gloria and what they felt about each other—there was to be a burial to give, and then the mourning of a brief life.

But Annette found no body beside the brush. The bundle of torn dress was gone, too, leaving only scraps behind. There were no signs that animals had taken the swaddled infant. The earth lay unbothered around her footprints from last evening and the slight groove where she had laid the baby.

She knelt anyway, reaching out for an absent soul. Even without a body, she could dig a symbolic grave, observe a burial of the scraps of dress. She could at least go through the respectful motions that any death deserved.

Her hands stretched ahead of her and froze in place. She had seen them in the glow of that other world, but a long time seemed to have passed since she saw them in true daylight.

Since the sun had last kissed her unmarked skin.

ACKNOWLEDGEMENTS

I'm tremendously grateful to everyone at Death's Head Press for their unflinching support of my angels and their cruelty. From concept to completion, they have had complete faith in my vision of this blasphemous, gory tale, from its colorful characters to its bloody massacres to its weird destinations and understandings. Jeremy, Anna, Steve, Kristy—thank you so much.

Fans of the Splatter Western series know that Justin Coons is a visionary. His cover art for *Cruel Angels Past Sundown* is a masterwork, and in my opinion, he's outdone himself.

I also want to thank Suzan Palumbo, Nat Cassidy, and Gabino Iglesias for their kind words toward me and my work.

Lastly, immense gratitude to my wife J. She has always supported me through every project great and small, but here she took on the loftier role of religious expert in doling out textual details and theological perspectives beyond what my upbringing could provide. This book is richer because of her. Thank you, J, for lighting the way

ABOUT THE AUTHOR

Hailey Piper is the Bram Stoker Award-winning author of *Queen of Teeth*, *No Gods for Drowning*, *Benny Rose the Cannibal King*, and *The Worm and His Kings* series, among other books of dark fiction. She is an active member of the Horror Writers Association, with short fiction appearing in *Pseudopod*, *Vastarien*, *Cosmic Horror Monthly*, Splatterpunk Award-winning anthology *Worst Laid Plans*, *Year's Best Hardcore Horror*, and other publications. She lives with her wife in Maryland, where their occult rituals are secret.

Find Hailey at www.haileypiper.com.